HIS VINYL VIXEN

A Beach Avenue Babes Romance

ABBY KNOX

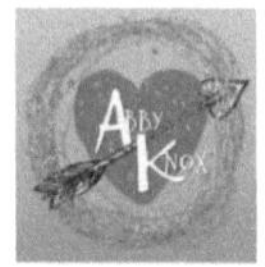

Edited by Aquila Editing

Cover Designer: Mayhem Cover Creations

Dedicated to the memory of the ultimate punk rock star, Anthony Bourdain, who left this earth while I was writing this book and listening to one of his favorite bands, The Ramones. My silly little heart will always be a little bit broken over you, Tony.

His Vinyl Vixen

Beach Avenue Babes, Part One

By Abby Knox

Zara Rhodes *is freshly graduated from her East Coast Ivy League college and has returned home to California, just for one summer. She's going to help out at her mother's struggling record store, and then split as soon as she finds her true calling. Having just turned 21, she should be sowing her wild oats. But she has no interest in making the same choices her mother did at that age. Which means, steering clear of men.*

Kai Stormcloud *is a a hippie drifter with a checkered past. He's starting over with only the guitar in his hands and his wits. Maybe he'll busk his way up the California coast until he's got enough money to send home to his aunt who raised him. Or, maybe follow his favorite jam band across the country for awhile. He doesn't know or care what happens after that. But when he spots a spunky little record store clerk on his first day in Sea Grove, he changes his tune. She makes it clear she doesn't trust his type, but Kai will do anything to win her over. Even get a real job.*

Chapter 1

Z *ara*

IF IT WERE possible to roll one's eyes in disgust before even opening them first thing in the morning, Zara Rhodes might achieve it with a flourish.

The seagulls called. The California sun shone down on Beach Avenue. The street performers strummed guitars and slapped bongos. All of the serene things of a quaint beach community conspired to wake Zara up too early from her slumber in the small flat she shared with her mother, Dusty.

Twenty-one years old and freshly graduated from college, Zara was not accustomed to waking up early. She was deeply entrenched in a season of life in which her body really, really enjoyed sleeping. A lot.

But she couldn't go back to sleep with the hippy-dippy music assaulting her. It was the sound of acoustic guitar out on the sidewalk, a sure sign that she was indeed home for the summer. The weather was getting hotter, and the buskers were starting early.

Well, shit.

Zara snapped the shade open with a testy flick of her wrist, as if taking out her anger on window coverings might give her any satisfaction before she had consumed any coffee. She looked down to the street and expected to find the old, familiar faces from last summer, with their threadbare Grateful Dead tee-shirts and Birkenstock sandals and graying, bleached-out beards.

But this one was new. She couldn't see his face because he was bent over while strumming a Martin N-20 acoustic guitar. *Good taste in instruments, anyway,* she thought. His hair was long and sandy, with random streaks of pure gold. He wore a pale woven Baja tunic that had seen better days. That 1990s relic of a garment probably reeked of pot, she thought.

Zara sighed. She didn't trust hippies.

She glanced at the hip-swaying Elvis clock on the wall. May as well get started early on work. *Mom's books are probably in disarray.* Zara dressed in her favorite plaid mini and fishnets. She had to look the part to sling records all day; yes, actual 12-inch vinyl records that were regularly bought up by retired, tanned baby boomers with too much money and time on their hands.

As she slipped through the great room she flipped on the stereo, where *Never Mind the Bollocks* by the Sex Pistols was already queued up. Zara padded into the kitchen, made coffee and poured it into her stainless mug. It had been a high school graduation gift on which she had immediately slapped on her favorite band stickers and scrawled it all over with anarchy symbols in permanent marker. Juvenile? Yes, but she thought it was a nice antidote for being a scholarship college student in possession of a $50 coffee mug.

Once in the bathroom applying her "look"—assertive lines of black kohl eyeliner and red lips—she heard her mother's footsteps come shuffling down the hall.

"Buskers are awake. Guess I better go open the store and help them make some money," Dusty said with a yawn and a smile.

"Ma, why do you put up with those guys? They're essentially panhandling for money right in front of your store. Which is, in case you forgot, a store that depends on you making actual money off the same people giving money to buskers."

Dusty cocked her head to one side and said, "Oh, Z, when are you gonna start calling me Dusty, like everyone else?"

Zara returned to penciling on her severe black eyeliner in the bathroom mirror. "When hell freezes over."

Dusty smoothed a hand over Zara's sleek dark locks. "You have such pretty hair." While Zara had a degree in economics, Dusty had a degree in non-sequiturs. "Wanna let me put some Dutch milkmaid braids in it?"

Zara moved on to her lips. She turned two tubes of lipstick upside down and read the names of the shades. *¡Olé!* and *Red Flag*. She was definitely feeling more *¡Olé!* today.

"Thank you. Hard pass on the milkmaid look," she said with a smirk.

Dusty shrugged. "Suit yourself." She turned sideways in the mirror next to her daughter. Dusty had a pretty banging figure at 42. "Bra or no bra today?"

"Ma."

"Oh come on, Z."

"Ma, nobody wants to see your nipples. Especially not on my birthday."

Dusty sucked in her belly. "You know, for an economics major, you understand very little about what sells vinyl records to a bunch of old rock music junkies. Nipples, baby. Nipples."

Zara blotted her lipstick and replied, "And now I'm scarred for life." She snapped the cap back on the lipstick and dropped it into her makeup bag. "OK. I'm gonna go open the shop. See you down there, slut."

Anybody else's mother would have been offended. Dusty was not anybody else's mother. Dusty called after Zara, "That's my girl! Oh, Happy 21st birthday, by the way!"

Zara called over her shoulder from the front door as she slipped into her Union Jack Doc Martens, "There'd better not be any cake; I'm off sugar!"

Dusty followed her into the great room and replied, "You know, just because you're in California doesn't mean anybody wants to hear about your diet. Excuse me, 'eating plan.' Ooh, coffee. Thank you!" And then a moment later she added, "That's was sarcasm. Everybody talks incessantly about their food plans these days, so you'll fit right in here."

Dusty gave her daughter a peck on the cheek. "Love you so much, sweetheart. Thank you for coming back after graduation."

Zara muttered but could not help the smile creeping across her lips. "Love you too, bye!"

She headed downstairs and thought, *At least I don't have a typical Southern California commute to work.* The storefront of Vinyl Vixen was literally underneath the walkup flat.

However, after Zara exited the staircase that led to the side street, she realized she did have to walk right past the two-tone blond busker and his guitar. She took a deep breath, resolved to avoid conversation with any new hippies at all costs, and marched around the corner to Beach Avenue. She tightened her grip on the set of keys laced through her fingers as precautionary little spikes of self-defense. Not that she would likely have to use her keys as a weapon on a mild-mannered guitar-playing beach bum in Sea Grove. But, one never knew. Best-case scenario, he would get the hint that she didn't want a new friend.

But, when she came around the corner, the busker wasn't there. *That's odd*, she thought. *Well, in my experience, they never stick around for long.*

And then all of a sudden, a man's deep voice came out of nowhere. "Walk of shame?"

Zara spun around. "Excuse me?"

The blond hippie dude was standing there with two cups of coffee in his hands and his guitar slung over his shoulder. He was taller than she had expected. And hotter. Way, way hotter. He had deep, soulful brown eyes and a built, sun-kissed chest that peeked through the opening in that god-awful woven tunic. He looked like a chill, California version of a Viking.

"I'm sorry," he said. "That was a joke."

Zara shook her head and mumbled, "Every-damn-body's got jokes today."

"Uhh…" the blond hippie man stammered. "I dunno what to say to that…"

Zara raised an eyebrow. "I'm shocked. Now, if you'll excuse me, I'll just rocket right past the Walk of Shame comment and go to work."

She turned away to unlock the front door, feeling deeply self-conscious knowing his eyes were on her back. He could not stop talking. Talking was not on the menu for

Zara before she finished her coffee. Not even talking to super-hot musicians.

"I…" he stammered. "I just meant that I saw you coming out of that apartment all dressed up and…never mind. This is for you."

Zara muscled the old wooden door open and peered at him. He was trying to hand off to her a paper cup of coffee from her favorite coffee spot, Voltaire's. She did not take it right away. "I have coffee," she said. She stood in the open doorway and gestured with her mug.

He looked like he wasn't sure himself what he was trying to do. "Oh, sorry. I'm Kai. I thought I would try to be a good neighbor and bring the manager of this fine historic music establishment a coffee, as a thank you for letting me busk here today."

Zara was confused. "I'm not a manager, I'm an associate. The owner will be down in a minute."

"But you do work here, right?"

"Yeah."

"So this is for you. Thank you." He held out the cup like he was a little boy holding up a perfect attendance certificate.

Zara thought this made him oddly that much cuter but kept her face stone cold. "First of all, you can't be here. Busking is bad for business. And second of all, what female in her right mind is going to take coffee from a total stranger? Ever heard of Rohypnol?"

"Yes."

"So, you'll understand if I say fuck off with your coffee."

He narrowed his gaze. "Do I look like a mustache-twirling bad guy to you?"

He didn't even appear defensive after her remark,

which intrigued Zara on the inside. On the outside, she sighed and rolled her eyes. "They never do."

He was grasping for something to reach her. "Seems we're getting off on the wrong foot." He put down the cup on the window sill. "Nice art," he said. On the other side of the plate glass window was Dusty's modern art palm tree sculpture made of little plastic adaptors for 45 records. He then held out his hand and said, "Let's try again. I'm Kai."

Kai. Total surfer name.

Zara smirked and hesitated before shaking that tanned, sinewy, musically talented hand. "Listen, Kai. Thank you for the coffee," she said, letting him take her hand. His fingers were warm but rougher than they ought to be at his age. "I don't think you're trying to roofie me. But busking is bad for business. It's glorified loitering."

"Well, Dusty said I could stay," he said with a smirk.

"Did she now?"

"Yep. I spoke to her last week. I guess that was before you arrived home from college."

What else had Dusty said to this total stranger about her? Zara studied his face. He was in his mid-30s, and definitely her mother's type. Dusty had always had a soft spot for hippies. Zara was suspicious. Her mom had been a bad picker. Exhibit A: Zara's own biological father, Walter. Inwardly, Zara shuddered and pushed the thought of that man out of her head.

She would have to watch out for this one. He had a kind face with a smile that reached his eyes, but that could be deceiving. Nice cheekbones and a nearly perfect aquiline nose of a marble Roman statue, but with added character. He'd clearly broken it a time or two. *There's definitely a story there.* The shaggy hair looked as if it had spent too much time in the surf. Total California babe, through and through. *Not my type,* said her left brain. *But you can't deny that something-something,* said her right brain.

"Fine," she said. "Just for today. And just so you know, if I decide I want you gone, you're gone. Dusty trusts my business decisions. And I don't trust hippies."

He looked amused. "I'm not a hippie."

She worked hard to contain a laugh. "Puka shell necklace, frayed hemp cargo shorts, woven tunic from 1993, Teva sandals, Buddhist bead bracelet. Keep telling yourself that."

"I'm not what you think. I'm just a guy with a guitar who likes to be close to the beach...and in close proximity to pretty, smart, punky-goth girls."

Zara felt a hot flush at that comment. Or it could have simply been the weather. Memorial Day temperatures were going to be hotter than usual this year. "Whatever, dude. Just don't bug the customers, OK?"

Kai saluted, causing Zara to roll her eyes again before grabbing the free coffee off the sill and heading to work.

Inside the store, she kept one eye on Kai through the window and one eye on selecting the soundtrack for her work day.

Rolling Stones? No. Beatles? No. Misfits? Maybe, maybe not. Michael Jackson? No.

Something in her brain told Zara to lean more toward Americana. *What the hell...Grateful Dead it is.*

Chapter 2

K *ai*

IT WAS Kai's first time in this coffee joint on Beach Avenue. As he waited in line, he noticed some cool framed quotes on the walls:

"Judge a man by his questions rather than by his answers."

"Let us read, and let us dance; these two amusements will never do any harm to the world."

Kai decided he was going to like this place.

He had arrived in town last week. It seemed like a cool locale to practice his music while earning a few bucks to send back home to his aunt.

Dusty had been very agreeable when he'd approached her about busking in front of her store, and had even hinted at having him help provide entertainment for a fundraiser for the local women's shelter.

"If you're any good," she'd said, with a no-nonsense expression.

Kai had known right away she was not a woman to be trifled with. And so he had decided to let her in on a little secret about his past. He hadn't come to California on a whim, but to try to put his past behind him. When the conversation ended, he was more or less a low-key security guard.

Just talking about these things made his mind flash back to the horrific scene last year. Black pavement, wet with rain. Blue lights flashing. Blood. Hot gun metal. Shock. A woman crying.

And so, Kai decided to kiss Dusty's ass a little by bringing her coffee as a thank-you gift. He liked Dusty, in that she reminded him of Aunt Jo, who'd raised him.

The notion of sucking up to Dusty that morning took a hasty back seat when Kai suddenly caught sight of the younger, scarier, more goth-punk version of Dusty that appeared out of nowhere.

That "walk of shame" comment was the wrong thing to say. He had blurted it out, trying to be funny, but immediately recognized it as totally inappropriate.

The way she spun around, it was as if he was being struck by lightning. She was college-age, wore knee-high Doc Marten boots that looked like she would kick the shit out of a dude as soon as talk to him. Fishnets under a plaid mini-skirt. Sexy black mesh top over a black concert tank top. Dark hair that gleamed rebelliously in the California sun. Lipstick the color of a fire engine and eyes that were not so much "come hither" as they communicated "fuck you." Eyebrow ring, nose ring. She carried a travel mug covered in anarchy symbols and '80s band stickers. This, he totally appreciated, having been raised by John Hughes and Molly Ringwald while he latchkeyed his way through childhood.

If he could speak to her without looking like a complete asshole, all the better. He quickly apologized and explained that he had bought her coffee.

After that, the conversation hadn't been too terrible. Even when she said, "fuck off with your coffee," she seemed to have been eyeing his guitar, and his chest.

She probably thinks I'm a hippie poseur who's got no talent whatsoever.

And why was he caring about her perception of him? Nobody had ever affected him that deeply on a first meeting. He never thought he cared for the hardcore punk aesthetic. But suddenly, he was coming around. Maybe it was her scent. Something about getting a whiff of her as she spun around had reminded him of special treats, like a kid getting surprise strawberry shortcake for breakfast.

She was so striking, he could come around on a lot of things. Pantomime. The word "slacks." Cheaply built McMansions. If he found out she liked any of those awful things, Kai would be the first in line for that bandwagon.

When she had consented to shake his hand, she felt cool to the touch, and it matched her overall cool, attractive, confident demeanor. But still, there was something else there. Her skin was impeccable, her hand felt soft and welcoming inside of his. Even as she was telling him that his favorite pastime, busking, was loitering, he sensed she didn't actually believe that. Or, that she was making an exception for him because she liked him. Whatever the reason, the little punk female was giving him hope.

After his encounter with Zara, Kai questioned his plan to stay in Sea Grove just long enough to earn a few bucks. He decided right then and there, that was a terrible plan.

He had no idea what the new plan was. Kai had never spoken to anyone quite like Zara in his whole life. Just one look at her had kicked the shit out of his heart, and he was happier for it.

Chapter 3

Z *ara*

DUSTY ENTERED the store smiling to herself, the doorbell signaling her presence with its sweet six-note chime that was only recognized by their most frequent customers as "Mama, I'm Coming Home."

"Good morning, Ozzy, hope you've been watching over my sweet baby Zara, hard at work," Dusty chirped.

Zara didn't want to know why she was so chipper and she wasn't going to ask. "You do know Ozzy is still alive, right?"

"Of course he is, doesn't mean I can't talk to him," Dusty replied, flipping around the "Open" sign.

Zara shook her head and continued working on getting her mother's books in order. Looking at the ledger, it was easy to see her mother was not a gifted bookkeeper. "What is 'bird banders' and why is there a debit of $50 next to this entry?"

Dusty was fingering her hair in the reflection of a Bad Company CD. "Oh come on, you know. It's when wildlife experts get together on the beach and put little bracelets on birds, so they can track the population. I mean, you're an Ivy League graduate, are you not? Aren't you the one who is supposed to be telling me what things are and are not?"

Zara took a beat to sip her coffee before she snapped back. She had switched to the coffee from Voltaire's. Her stainless mug sat by the register, ignored.

Voltaire's coffee was good. House blend, cream, no sugar. It was a good thing Kai had not given this coffee for Dusty, because she liked sugar.

"Mom, I know what bird banding is. I'm asking you, why would Vinyl Vixen, a record store that is not exactly comfortably in the black at this moment, have an entry in the ledger for bird banding?"

Dusty set about opening a box of something that had just come in from the parcel service. She attacked it carefully with box cutters. "Well, it is a good idea to record your donations, is it not? I thought you would be proud of me for remembering to do that. You know, like a tax write-off? Ooh, yay, the new Foo Fighters on vinyl! I have an online customer waiting for this; god knows why he orders from little ol' me. Goddamn, I would leave this all behind if that scruffy Dave Grohl ever came walking through this door. Beach Avenue? See ya! Wouldn't wanna be ya!"

"Dave Grohl is like, intensely married, mother. And also, you have no business giving to charity in that amount. Do you have a receipt?"

Dusty turned off the Grateful Dead on the stereo and replaced it with one of her old blues-guitar stand-bys, Jed "Big Daddy" Masters. Jed always put a dreamier look on her face than even the Foo. She swayed to the roaring guitar licks with her eyes closed, like a wanna-be groupie.

"Hmm? Receipt?" Dusty said absently. "Hey, you know, I wonder if old Jed is married? I bet he's a sly one. You know, I've never been a mistress, maybe I should give it a try. They say you should do one thing that scares you every day."

Zara clicked her mechanical pencil on the glass counter that encased a collection of signed concert memorabilia. One was a pair of eyeglass frames that resembled Buddy Holly's. Zara looked at the frames and wondered why her mother would never have them appraised and put up for sale. She could certainly use the money, if they were real. But, there was no way they could be authentic. *They would have to be in the Smithsonian, wouldn't they?*

Zara sighed and rubbed her eyes. Then her eyes fell on to Dusty's smart phone that was propped up against the register. Zara picked it up and checked the battery life. Dead. As always. She plugged it into a charger for her.

"Ma, can we focus please? Why do you have an entry for bird banding in the ledger?"

"Every spring those scientists come to town to do their thing with the birds nesting on the beach, and I gave them all vouchers. You never know, they could be back this way for vacation over the summer and now they'll have money to spend."

"*Your* money to spend. And also, that's not a charitable donation, but it's decent marketing. That is tax deductible. But you need to find the receipt. And you have to keep better records. Every cent you give away should be carefully accounted for."

Big Daddy howled over the speaker system and Dusty clomped over in her Frankenstein-platform boots to kiss her daughter on the forehead. "You're so smart. I love you."

"Love you too." Zara pointed to Dusty's smartphone. "But I wish you wouldn't leave your phone down here overnight."

Dusty shrugged. "You know those things confuse me. I would much rather talk to people on a land line. It's way sexier. The sound quality is totally different. It's like listening to an mp3 versus a record. Digital has no soul!"

Zara struggled not to roll her eyes. She had heard this speech way too many times.

Fortunately, Dusty jumped to yet another topic. "So what are we doing for your big birthday?"

"It's not a big deal. I'm only 21."

"You're kidding me, right? We need to go out and party!" Dusty exclaimed, miming a bottle-drinking gesture with both her hands.

"You know I'm not much of a drinker, Ma."

Dusty eyed her daughter. "Baby girl, when I was your age, I was tearing it up with my friends. That summer after high school graduation, we were partying on the beach every night."

Zara watched Dusty put the new Foo Fighters stack of vinyl under "G" for "Grunge." Zara walked over to correctly file them under hard rock. The Foo Fighters had far outlived grunge.

"Yeah, well, I graduated a year early and I didn't like anybody at my high school, so I sorta missed all of the local yokel hootenannies."

Dusty laughed. "Yeah, you've always been your own person, and I love that about you, babe. But you do have a pulse, as far as I can tell. If I were you, I certainly wouldn't be stuck inside a shop all day long. I'd be outside flirting with that cute young thing out there who's making googly eyes at you right now, playing Johnny Cash."

Zara, before thinking, darted her eyes toward the plate glass window. On the other side, Kai was staring straight at her while loudly singing the chorus to "Ring of Fire." The eye contact made her stomach flip, and Dusty caught it.

"Go talk to him!" Dusty said.

Zara blushed. She wished her mother would stay out of her love life. She flipped the ledger closed and shoved it into a metal filing cabinet, slamming it shut. "Because flirting with random hippies worked out really well for you at 21."

Dusty's eyes widened at this cruel remark. "Really?"

Zara realized her emotional confusion had made her lash out at her mom and she instantly regretted it.

"Ma, I'm so sorry. I didn't mean it like that."

Dusty shrugged and set about dusting and straightening. "It's fine, baby. And it's true. But remember, you wouldn't have all this luxury at your disposal without me." Dusty gestured around the shop with a wide wave of her arm. "Including the water-stained ceiling and lead-painted windows! It's all yours in the will, princess!"

Zara laughed. "OK, let me make it up to you. I'll let you take me out for my 21st birthday."

Dusty laughed and wandered over to the outdated computer behind the front counter, plonking herself down in the aging office chair. "Oh, you have no choice in the matter, we are doing that either way. But what you *can* do is help me organize the block party for the Fourth of July."

Zara gave her usual attitude about community events. "Oh yay. Fourth of July. Fireworks. Kids. Meat. Fire. Outdoors. Excellent."

Dusty smiled. "Thank you so much, babe. You are my favorite daughter."

Zara shook her head. "Well, if you were gonna have another one you better get started now."

"Yeah right, with who?"

"I don't know, the parcel carrier seems to dig you."

Dusty squinted at the screen and tapped the keyboard. "Honestly I don't trust myself in a relationship with any man other than my reclusive e-mail customers, whom I'll never meet in real life. Not after everything that happened with your dad."

"Oh, Mom. Give yourself some credit. You did manage to not raise me in a teepee."

"Barely. Ah, finally, here's that blasted flier I was working on."

"Since I was seven. It counts."

"Still feels like yesterday since I woke up to all your dad's shenanigans." She tapped on the keyboard and made some edits to the Fourth of July party flier.

Zara peered over her mother's shoulder. "Yeah, well, it's ancient history, and Walter is not exactly worthy of the 'Dad' title while sitting in prison."

"You know he's still making fake profiles on social media to stalk me and telling everyone that I bankrupted an entire non-profit group of peace activists."

Her father's antics knew no bounds — not even from prison — and it made Zara angry thinking about it. "The people who really know you know the truth. If anyone else doesn't see how amazing you are, then fuck them."

"Zara!" Dusty spun around in her chair with a shocked look on her face.

"Oh, what, you want me to call you by your first name like you're such a cool mom, but you're gonna get scandalized and grab your pearls because I use a cuss word that I have heard you using daily since birth?"

"I'll have you know it's a spiked leather choker, not pearls. And yes. You are a lady."

Zara sipped her coffee but grinned. "I may be a lady, but I learned how to cuss from the best of the ladies."

As she smiled at her mother, she looked over her shoulder and stole a glance at Kai through the front window to where he was playing to a group of teenagers.

She could tell Kai had been staring again but had looked away when she looked his way. He was strumming his way through an acoustic version of "Smells Like Teen Spirit." Zara could not keep herself from grinning in approval.

Just then, one of their regular customers, Ben from Orange County, walked in. Music geeks and old-timers all over Southern California sought this place out. Sometimes just to shoot the shit with Dusty and Zara.

So, it was a good thing Zara had been in love with music since the time she could walk. As a result, her mother employed her as a bit of a parlor trick to impress the hardcore collectors.

On this day, Ben said nothing, but walked right up to Zara and hummed a few bars of a chorus. Zara took this as her cue that he was trying to locate a certain song, but he couldn't remember the name of it or who sang it. She listened to Ben for about 15 seconds, then sighed and muttered, "'Goodnight Sweet Josephine.' Yardbirds. Filed under Y in overrated 1960s wannabe psychedelic music. Over there."

Dusty scoffed. "A bit judgmental, Zara?"

Zara shrugged. "Ben can handle it."

Ben shrugged, nodded in agreement and made his way over to peruse the oddly specific section of vintage records.

Speaking of filing systems, Zara needed to check on the store's crowning achievement. She walked over to another massive filing cabinet and pulled open one drawer. She breathed a sigh of relief.

Dusty smiled. "Don't worry, angel. I didn't even touch your files. It's all just as you left it."

Zara seemed satisfied, then turned to her mother. "Yes, but did you file the actual music according to the system I have set up in the cabinet?"

"No comment," replied Dusty.

Zara shut the drawer a little louder than necessary and pinched the bridge of her nose. She breathed, and Dusty continued. "Besides, what does it matter? You are a snob. A music snob and a genius who can practically smell which song a customer is looking for the second they walk in."

Zara gave another signature eye roll. "True enough. Guess I've got all summer to sort it out again."

Dusty sighed. "Well, that sounds like super-awesome fun in the sun. You know, they make medicine for OCD people such as yourself."

But Zara was ignoring Dusty's comments, because someone else was catching her eye again. Kai was now somehow managing to vamp his way from Nirvana into "(You Make Me Feel Like) A Natural Woman" by Aretha Franklin. She laughed. She had to admit he had a good sense of humor and a nice enough singing voice.

Then she caught herself smiling directly at him and turned away.

Back to work, Zara.

Chapter 4

K *ai*

FOUR DAYS into his summer vacation—or whatever this was—and the shy smiles from the girl in the scary boots were coming at him with increasing frequency. That was something. He had made the terrifyingly hot girl smile.

But was she a goth girl? A punk girl? Hardcore? Something in between? Soon enough, he would find out. Not like he was overly concerned what she identified as. As long as very soon she could identify as his girlfriend.

Girlfriend.

He liked the sound of that.

Don't get ahead of yourself, man. She doesn't really like you. She already said she doesn't trust hippies. And she sure isn't gonna like your whole complete backstory.

But over the Memorial Day weekend, he had seen that shy smile more often than he had seen her punk girl scowl.

As it happened, the holiday foot traffic on Beach Avenue had been pretty lucrative. But even if he'd made zero dollars in tips, just seeing her look at him like that felt like he'd made a platinum record.

The holiday had come and gone, and now it was June. He had made bank with the crowd pleasers. This morning, Kai was breaking out his truly favorite things to play. Crosby, Stills, Nash & Young. Pink Floyd. Even threw some prog rock and yacht rock in there from time to time. What could he say? He enjoyed him some Michael McDonald and Doobie Brothers.

For the morning after Memorial Day, he was doing pretty well in tips. He was starting to get hungry, so he counted up his take so far. He had just enough to get something really special for Zara for lunch.

Just then, Dusty stepped outside and Kai enthusiastically wailed the first few bars of "Crazy Train" on his guitar.

"You know me well," she said with a grin, handing him a bottled water. "Just wanted you to know my store's receipts are up from the last two Memorial Day weekends, and Zara thinks it has something to do with you."

He smiled and stopped playing to take the bottle. "She does?" He sounded a little too excited and corrected himself. "I mean, oh, yeah? She does? I mean, that's cool. I wouldn't want to, you know, drive traffic away."

Dusty smiled knowingly and watched him drink his water. Kai could tell she wanted to say something else.

"How would you like a real job?"

That was not what he was expecting her to say. He was expecting her to say something like, *If you break my daughter's heart I will break your face.* But that was pretty well implied just being around those two.

"A job?"

Dusty nodded. "Look, I know what we talked about before. And I still want you to be on the lookout for unsavory characters while you're here. But, I just wondered if there was any chance you'd be interested in…staying. Taking a real job. Hanging around."

Kai caught her meaning completely. She was full of surprises. "Yeah," he said, his smile broadening. "Yeah, I'd love a job. I mean, I'd want it keep playing if I could—and watching out for the other stuff we talked about—but I'll do whatever you need me to do."

"That's good to know, because I have to leave town for a couple of days. I haven't told Zara, but I'm gonna be taking a little vacation. She can run the place just fine, but we'll need an extra pair of hands. And eyes. And ears. I don't want her in the shop by herself. And I'd love for you to agree to provide entertainment for this Fourth of July block party I'm hosting. I'm making it a fundraiser for the women's shelter in Sand Hill."

Kai was bowled over but tried not to sound too enthusiastic about the idea of being alone in the shop with Zara. "Whatever you need. Put me to work. In fact, do you need a stage? I can build you one." So much for playing it cool.

Dusty looked pleasantly surprised. "Really? Wow, that's great! You're a good man, Kai, thank you." She put out her hand and shook his. "Glad to have you on board. Zara will be your point person on party planning, so any questions, just go straight to her."

Kai thought this could not have worked out any better.

"Hey, why don't I go ahead and pick up lunch for the three of us and we can start planning right away."

Dusty seemed overjoyed. "I love your initiative."

Kai smiled. "Remember, I'm just a guy with a guitar who likes to be useful."

Dusty winked.

Chapter 5

Z *ara*

HOW HAD this guy figured her out already? How did he just…*get* her?

Last week, he'd brought her her favorite coffee. Then, all through Memorial weekend, he broke into song whenever she passed by, specifically into a variety of 1980s romantic prog-rock songs like "Your Love" by the Outfield and "Pretty in Pink" by the Psychedelic Furs. He seemed to share her affinity for John Hughes soundtracks. She didn't let him know that she appreciated it. How did he know she had a gushy side? She thought she hid it so well.

Not that any of this was working on her. *No. Not working at all. Nope.*

And then, today, Kai had picked up lunch from her favorite vegan place and returned to the record store with a sack full of salads, gluten-free pitas and hummus.

She wasn't sure if she could trust a guy who was so obviously into her. But, she had no other choice as Dusty, over lunch, had announced she was taking a mini vacation to go "find herself." When Zara had countered with the fact that Dusty hardly had income to support a vacation at the moment, Dusty explained she was just going to stay with her old high school best friend, Marti, in Santa Barbara for a few days. "Just to sit on the beach and think, away from work. You know how it is."

"And tell me again why you think it's a good idea to leave me alone with a drifter in the shop?" Zara whispered between clenched teeth as she followed her mother to the car, hoping to hell it was out of earshot from Kai. Not that she cared if she hurt his feelings. *Nope. Not at all.*

"I checked him out, Zara. Don't you think I would? No record. Legit Social Security Number. I even called his auntie in Oregon. Everything checks out."

Well, what could Zara say to the woman who had raised her on her own? She couldn't exactly stand in front of her car. And besides, she rarely did a thing for herself. A little getaway was in order.

After seeing her mother off, Zara sat on a stool outside the record store while Kai played. It was a pleasant day and the sun wasn't too brutal. Plus, there was that after-noon slump. There wouldn't be many customers again until after dinner.

"I feel guilty sitting on your stool while you play," Zara said to Kai.

"Shawty, I don't mind," he sang, winking at her.

"Now you know Usher?"

"A little."

"Why are you being so nice to me?" she asked.

"Because you're letting me," he replied. "*Breakfast Club!*"

And then the Usher song was over and Kai was launching into "Don't You Forget About Me," and it wasn't even that weird of a transition.

"How do you do that?" she said, showing him something between a sneer and a smirk, shaking her head and returning to the legal pad she was using to brainstorm ideas for the Fourth of July party.

"You bring it out in me, I guess," he answered.

Zara cleared her throat and examined the list. So far on the to-do list, Kai had committed to building a small stage for entertainment, handing out fliers, and setting up a misting station for partiers to cool themselves, and arranging for security.

She would submit a request for a permit from the City of Sea Grove to block off the block of Beach Avenue for the party. They would put Dusty and her in charge of decorations and recruiting food trucks.

Between songs, Kai added, "Are we selling tickets to this shindig?"

"I don't know. Mom just said it was a block party. She didn't give me many parameters. Rules and parameters aren't exactly her thing."

Kai laughed. "Yeah, I picked up on that. What is her thing?"

"Well, she's really good at being a mom."

Kai smiled. "Obviously. She made you."

Zara felt herself blush a little. "Well, she didn't raise me under the best of circumstances, but she pulled it together and we ended up in a good place. I just wish she would look at the record store as more of a business investment and not a vanity project."

Kai nodded thoughtfully. "But she's an artist. You're the business person. You make a good team."

"What do you mean, she's an artist?"

Kai gestured with his yellow guitar pick to the store window. She studied the sculpture of melted 45 adapters in the shape of a giant palm tree. There was also the miniature surf-hut constructed out of record jackets.

"Dusty made that display, didn't she? She's crazy talented."

Zara had never thought about the store window displays as more than her mother's pulling something out of her ass. But then again, Dusty was pretty good with making fliers and concert posters for all the local bands that played nearby. She did all that stuff voluntarily, though, and refused to take a dime for any of it.

"You know what? You're right. I just wish she could parlay that artistic brain of hers into some real money. Sometimes I think she's just keeping the store open to appease the 15 crusty old guys who come by to get their plastic hoarding fix."

Kai nodded and looked out to the sidewalk. A gaggle of females in midriff tops and flip-flops were about five stores away. Zara could tell he was thinking of what to play next.

"You never know," Kai said. "Maybe one day somebody super famous will walk into the store and put this place on the map."

Zara considered this idea. "Even though I'm a wound-up ball of existential dread, I have to say I like your optimism, Kai."

But Kai was thinking about the music and watching the gaggle of women.

Zara sighed internally and turned to look at them. They were headed their way. She surmised they were in their early 40s and had been to several wine tastings already today. She looked back at Kai. She could see a light dawn in his eyes.

And then, sure as shit, Zara knew exactly what song he was going to play.

As the ladies approached, about one block away, Kai started strumming the first few measures of that one classic song. That one and only swoon-inducing number that would draw all the women of a certain age to flock to guys with guitars at parties.

"Saying I lo-ove you is not the words I want to hear from you…"

Zara could not help it. She fought it, but it was a losing battle. On the outside, she was rolling her eyes. On the inside, she totally melted inside her Doc Martens. "More than Words" by Extreme. Dammit. Why would this amount of commercial cheese work on her?

Normally, she would have said adios and bolted out of there. If a hippie in a Baja pullover had whipped out his guitar at a party and started playing this song back East at college, Zara would exit stage left just in time for all the other females to swoop in like a festival of swoons.

And yet. He sang this song like an absolute angel. The guitar playing was simple and showed off his voice better than any song he normally played. It was beautiful. Despite herself, despite everything she stood for, it was making her hot.

One of the women put her hand over hear heart as he sang. "Oh my gawd," the woman said when he had finished. "That was the first dance at my wedding."

Zara handed some fliers to the women.

"Kai," she said, when they had left.

"What?" he asked.

"You are wasting your time."

"What do you mean?"

"You have a really fucking good singing voice. You should be recording."

"Why?" He looked incredulous. As if he really didn't know.

Zara pushed. "So people can know you. So they can buy your records and you can stop busking and working at a record store."

Kai smiled. "But people are hearing me. That's enough for me."

Zara was confused. "But what people? Tourists?"

He smirked at her sideways as he tuned up his guitar. "No. You. Just you. That's enough for me."

Chapter 6

K *ai*

KAI REALLY WASN'T the party-planning type, but then he really wasn't the anything-planning type.

He could see Zara was very much into planning. She was a regulator. She was wound as tight as a guitar string, and he wanted to be the one to help her let loose.

He had made headway with that comment about her being enough for him. She looked unsettled as he locked onto her eyes. Unsettled with an edge of lust. She revealed it by biting her luscious bottom lip.

He couldn't wait to kiss it.

He was going to kiss it tonight, he decided.

"Why don't we continue this planning meeting tonight over dinner?" he asked.

Zara looked at him suspiciously. "Where?"

Kai looked around. "I don't know. Maybe Angelo's?"

Zara laughed. You want to meet and talk party planning over a fancy dinner on the pier? Are you asking me on a date?"

Kai immediately manned up. "Yes. It's a date if you want it to be a date. If you don't want it to be a date, then it doesn't have to be."

He watched as Zara licked her lips. He could see he was making her blush again. This was a good sign.

"I don't date hippies. But I'll have a meeting with you."

Kai shrugged and started picking aimlessly on his guitar, trying to decide what to play next. "You know, we're not all the same."

Zara smiled. "I know. I just had a really bad, weird—I don't really want to talk about it. Let's just say my dad was…well, it's a long story. Suffice it to say, I'm extremely careful around men."

Kai nodded and recalled his own Aunt Jo's most recent poor choice in men. He shook off the memory and the dark clouds associated with all of that and strummed the opening chords to "The Man Who Sold the World."

"That's for you," he said as she stood up to back inside. "I know you like Nirvana."

THE 40-SOMETHING CUSTOMER with the tweed cap and the flannel shirt was getting on Zara's nerves. That much, Kai could tell.

"It sounds like Smashing Pumpkins but tighter," the customer was saying. Kai was examining the water stain in the drop ceiling but also listening intently.

"Tighter?" Zara asked, with an edge to her voice.

"Yeah. And better," the customer replied.

"Better?"

Uh oh, thought Kai. *I should say a prayer for that dude right now.*

"You're judging me," the customer said.

She cocked her head and said sarcastically, "Am I?"

"OK, let me see if I can hum it…" the man said.

She crossed her arms and listened. "Will the rock gods please send me a real challenge? It's 'Lazy Eye' by Silversun Pickups. And how dare you say they're tighter than Smashing Pumpkins. First of all, they're not even in the same league," Zara said, as if she was a fire-and-brimstone preacher just getting ramped up for the big sermon.

"Great! Where's your alternative section?"

She sighed and closed her eyes, taking a moment to pinch the bridge of her nose. "You're kidding me, right? We don't have alternative. We have rock, hard rock, punk, skater punk, metal, emo, prog rock, indie rock, electronica, house, lo-fi, chill-wave, grunge and within grunge we have Sub Pop Records. The list goes on and on. Alternative is an illusion. It's a label that means nothing."

"So…"

"It's in Y2K-era indie rock, over there," she said, pointing the man to the appropriate section.

When the customer nodded and walked away to find his record, Kai mused at her from his position on top of the ladder.

"Alternative is an illusion, that's deep," he said.

"The word annoys me, so I came up with another system," she said with a shrug and went to re-order the Shawn Colvin in order of year of release.

Kai shone a flashlight into the dark void above the drop ceiling, looking for the source of the leak. He said, "But you're filing that one in alt-country."

She said, "It's a much more specific, homogenous brand and encompasses a group of artists that complement each other. Alternative rock is nonsense."

Kai nodded. "OK. Explain." He hopped down from the ladder, leaning against it as he listened, arms crossed.

"OK, so if it's got electric guitar and drums and minimal electronics, it's rock."

"The Shins?"

"Rock."

"The Yeah Yeah Yeahs?"

"Rock."

"Led Zeppelin?"

"Classic rock."

"Ah," Kai said, lifting his index finger like he was going to try to out-nerd her. "But what is classic? That's about as nebulous as alternative."

Zara stated as a matter of fact, "Rock music created post 1968, pre-1985, primarily comprised of aforementioned instruments and minimal pop influence."

"But who says it has to be that? Who says Duran Duran isn't classic rock because it's from the 1980s?"

"That's pop," she said.

"Based on what?"

She looked up at the ceiling and thought about her answer. "Commercially driven, teen idols, more concerned with image than with musical quality…"

He continued to push. "So it's not even rock? Seems to me they have a drummer and two decent guitarists."

Zara shook her head. "The amount of dated 1980s electronic keyboard, plus their brand—the hair, the makeup, the videos full of supermodels—it all reads as pop. They are also cross-referenced as yacht rock."

"By who?" Kai said.

"By me," she answered, as if it was obvious she was the final authority.

"How can you put them in the same category as the Doobie Brothers?"

"It's only cross-referenced like that because of 'Rio.' You know, the video with the yacht."

He threw his back and howled with laughter. "That's crazy!"

She shrugged. "You know me. I like to throw caution to the wind. Odd cross-references are my favorite pastime."

She rang up the customer who found the recording he was looking for. When he left, she grabbed her keys to lock up for the night and announced she would be going upstairs to prep for their date. But first, she approached Kai and gave him a killer arched eyebrow. "And I do like that Nirvana song. But Bowie's version is better, as you well know."

Kai agreed with her completely as he watched her leave and round the corner. He hated having to wait for her to get ready, but hell, he didn't mind watching her cute little ass walk away. He silently congratulated himself. He had a date with Zara.

KAI COULD NOT HELP but smile as he watched this woman put away her crab legs.

It was nice to sit quietly and look at her, talk to her, and not have to think about earning his next tip.

"I'm surprised you decided to take a permanent job here. You strike me more as an adherent to the gig economy," she said.

Kai set down his fork, folded his hands on the table in

front of him and leaned in. He looked her square in the eyes so she would understand he was being totally serious. "For you. I got a job because I want to stay here and get to know you."

Chapter 7

Z *ara*

HER HEART BEGAN RACING. The heat was reddening her cheeks like a signal fire, and the self-awareness of her redness made the red grow even deeper. Her blood pulsed all the way up to her ears.

She took a drink of water.

"Kai," she started, barely able to meet his eyes. "You're expecting a lot of me that I don't know if I can deliver."

The truth was, she was flattered. Nobody had ever done anything to try to impress her before.

"Zara. You're scary smart. I can talk to you about Jimi Hendrix and The Weeknd in the same breath. You're amazingly hot and you don't even know it. You're funny. And goddamn, you are killing me in your combat boots and tiny skirts every day. Everything about you makes me feel like I'm just waking up to my real life. And all I want to do is spend all my time with you, if you'll let me."

Zara felt a certain energy move back down into her stomach, down her legs, all the way down to her toes. Nobody had ever pursued her before.

"You do know I just turned 21. I'm a bit younger than you."

"Ten years. That's nothing. How was your birthday, by the way?"

She smiled and cracked open another crab leg. "It was good. Mom got a little tipsy during the brew-and-view screening of *Plan 9 From Outer Space.* Then we just walked around some, got some ice cream. It was nice. I kind of forgot this town can be fun. I've pretty much spent the last four years on lockdown trying to maintain my scholarships."

Kai smiled. "You forgot that the sunny beach town of Sea Grove, with its boardwalks, festivals, art galleries, coffee shops, kickass food, and a music store owned by your own mother can conceivably be a fun place to live?"

Zara squinted. "I'm picking up the sarcasm, my friend."

Kai leaned back in his chair and stared. He looked like he was having a mischievous thought. "Speaking of fun, I've got an idea."

Zara looked at him and was not sure she trusted that look on his face. "I'm pretty sure my idea of fun and your idea of fun are different. As in, your idea of fun would probably fart in the general direction of my idea of fun."

Kai shrugged. "Well, there's nobody in this world who doesn't love karaoke, so I think that could be where our Venn diagrams intersect."

She smirked. "I think you overstate the universal appeal of karaoke."

He reached into his pocket and peeled off a couple dozen single bills, slapping them on the table. Clearly he was paying from his tip jar for the day. This made her heart feel a little sad. Kai caught her look of sympathy. "It's my money, and I can handle it. Let's go."

She allowed Kai to hold her hand as they walked their way down off the pier and back across Beach Avenue to the Sing Noodle House.

"What are we doing here? We just ate," she asked.

"On Tuesday nights they do karaoke. Haven't you lived here for your whole life?"

"Kinda."

"How is it possibly you've never been here for karaoke?"

"Trivia night is more my speed," she said. "I try to put on my cloak of invisibility when people want me to make a spectacle out of myself."

Kai stopped before reaching for the door. Without warning, he pulled Zara in close and wrapped his arms around her waist.

His eyes searched her face; his lips were inches away from hers. His arms squeezed around her in a way that was too familiar, but she felt her body soften. What the fuck did he think he was doing?

"Don't worry, I'm not going to kiss you yet," he said, as if reading her mind. "I'm just going to tell you that it doesn't matter what you do, how much you try to hide, you are the center of attention everywhere you go. Because you are fucking amazing. And you deserve all the attention."

"Kai," she heard herself say, the word coming out awkwardly as she looked around. "People are staring at you."

"No, they're staring at you. Because you're beautiful

and sweet and terrifying all wrapped up in a cool little package that lets nobody see the real you."

She scoffed. "I prefer to think of it as my own personal panic room."

"What are you panicking about?"

"I don't sing in front of people. Why are you making me do this?"

He sighed. "Because if we're going to spend time together, this is one of the things we're going to do."

"Who says I want to spend time with you?" There went her smartass mouth again.

She could see the wheels turning. She looked into his eyes to see if she'd hurt him. But honestly, she didn't see any hurt. She saw determination.

Men usually gave up on her after the first "fuck you and your free coffee." That suited her just fine.

Most men were weak. Her biological father was weak.

Kai was not most men. He was undeterred by her resting bitch face.

Chapter 8

K *ai*

HE HAD TAKEN A HUGE RISK, grabbing her like that. She was rigid at first, and Kai thought she might bolt. But then to his relief, she relaxed. She felt right in his arms, and as necessary as one of his own limbs.

He had no business putting his hands on this female whom he had only just met last week and who was now his coworker and the daughter of his boss. The inappropriateness of this contact with her made it all the more interesting. She felt it, too. She glared at him, but her cheeks were turning pink and her pupils were dilating. Her body was responding to him, even if the solid coat of steel around her heart was not.

He released her from his grip and took her hand. In her eyes he saw relief and surprise, but maybe also a little bit of disappointment. Had she wanted him to kiss her?

He grinned. "You've been working hard. It's time to loosen up."

Inside, he moseyed up to the bar where the bartender already had a Budweiser cracked open for him and waiting. "Hello, my friend."

Kai nodded. "How's it hangin', Chan?"

Zara looked at him in amazement.

"What?" Kai asked, feeling self-conscious.

"You've lived here a week and you already know the name of everyone in town?"

He shrugged and asked her what she wanted to drink.

"Seltzer, please."

The bartender eyed her suspiciously then looked at Kai. Kai placated him with, "She's my designated driver tonight, cut her some slack."

Zara took her seltzer and followed Kai to a table right in front of the stage. "I'm not singing, I don't care what you say."

"Oh, but you do," he replied, waggling his eyebrows at her mischievously.

"Well, yes I do, but it's a free country and I don't have to sing."

"But what if I said I really, really wanted to hear you sing?"

She sighed. "OK, but I don't want you giving me a hard time about the song."

He smiled. "No Sex Pistols. You gotta pick something that 100 percent of people like. The key here is short, peppy and popular. No The Smiths either."

Zara rolled her eyes. "What, you don't think 'Meat is Murder' will be perky enough?"

Kai was falling for this sassy female beyond all reason. The truth was, he didn't need her to sing. He already could see into her and she belonged to him. Body and soul. She had a fire in her belly and an attitude to match it. He desired everything about her. He just wanted to be close to her, even if she could not carry a tune in a bucket. Her mind, her humor, her smartass comments. Her sweet and salty little sneer. Every time she gave him that sideways sarcastic lip he wanted to bite it. He wanted to shock her by running his hands right up under that little plaid skirt of hers.

Well, he thought, it was dark in there, and there were tablecloths long enough to hide any illicit behavior that might be going on from the waist down. *Let's just see how things go first, lover boy,* he thought.

Chapter 9

Z *ara*

SHE DRANK her seltzer and he drank his beer. They talked, and she realized she had spent the entire day with him and didn't feel the urge to punch him in the throat.

She could easily fall for this boy. He had a functioning brain when it came to music. He knew how to cheer her up with coffee and food. She liked the way he smelled. And even more, the way he looked at her. He was kind and polite in all the right ways. He had a beautiful singing voice.

But Dusty had fallen for a guy with a similar mystique when she was precisely the age Zara was now, and that had changed Dusty's entire life trajectory.

Zara needed to know more things before he touched her again. She didn't trust herself to put on the brakes.

"I need to ask you something," she said.

"OK."

"There's a reason I don't trust hippie-bohemian types. Tell me more about yourself. I'll know if you're lying."

"I have no reason to lie."

"Sure you do. You're trying to woo me. So therefore anything you say can be construed as an embellishment in order to win me over. So spill it. Are you a serial killer? Do you live in a tent? What's your deal?"

Kai laughed. "I'm not a serial killer. I'm very good looking and I don't have a comb-over or pop-bottle glasses."

She glowered at him and set him straight. "Women found Ted Bundy to be very attractive. No comb-over."

"Ah yes, but he used crutches and pretended to be helpless, didn't he?"

"Very true," she said. "You're definitely not helpless. I'm just having a hard time deciding what my guts are telling me."

Kai studied her face so intently she felt self-conscious. Finally, he dug out his canvas wallet.

"That thing looks like you made it at summer camp," she said.

"I did," he said, in that proud-little-boy way that made Zara melt.

He literally laid out all his cards on the table. Then took a big swallow of beer while she inspected them.

Among the cards on the table was his legit-looking driver license. The only thing that seemed fake was his name. "Kai Stormcloud? Come on."

"Real hippie parents," he said with a shrug, pulling on his beer. "Changed their last name and everything."

Zara's dad had been a right asshole, but at least he

didn't saddle her with an ultra-hippie name. Looking back down at the table, she noticed he had no health insurance cards, which did not surprise her. No credit cards or debit cards, oddly.

"I do have some concerns here," she said. "First of all, I don't see a library card. Second of all, you should not be walking around with your social security card. If you get robbed, it's all the easier to steal your identity."

"OK. Tomorrow I'll get a library card for our next date," he said with sincerity.

"Who says we're having a next date?"

Kai leaned in and murmured close to her face, "Because if things go well, I hope tomorrow will just be a continuation of this date."

"You're making me blush."

"And you're making me really fuckin' hot."

Zara was feeling flushed and took a long sip of her cold seltzer to calm herself down.

"So, what's your story, Kai?"

"I was raised by my aunt in Oregon. Long story. Both my parents are alcoholics who sort of wandered off and left me with her. She's my absolute hero. I worship the ground she walks on. She always let me be who I was. I asked for guitar lessons, she made sure it happened even though she never had much money. Every cent I make, half of it goes back to my aunt. Her husband was a tool, never supported her desire to go back to school. Really controlling. He's dead now, may he not rest in peace."

Zara had the feeling he was telling the truth. "When was the last time you saw her?"

"Last year. I lived with her longer than a grown man should live with his mom or aunt. But I helped her around the house and I worked. A lot.

"But then last year she said, 'Kai, you need to go find yourself and see the rest of the country.' I said I wanted to stay and take care of her, but she insisted. So, I scraped money together, gave her half of it and used the rest to make my way down to San Diego. Since then, I've been going from place to place, busking, staying in motels when I can afford it, or staying with friends I make along the way. A few months here. A few weeks there. And that's about it. But now that I found you, I don't really feel like leaving Sea Grove. In fact, I'm moving into my own apartment next week."

She studied his face. He was telling the truth. "I don't know what to say to that. It's a big step to commit to an apartment at Southern California rental prices based on a feeling about a girl."

"More than a feeling," he said.

"Boston. Good song," she said.

"Seriously. I have money saved. You don't need to worry about me."

Zara drew in a shaky breath. "Well, since you spilled your guts, it's only fair to tell you about my trust issues."

"Go on."

"My mom fell for my father when she was 21. She was sort of a grass-roots groupie, followed his little unknown band from place to place. Eventually, he got her pregnant, but he seemed cool with the idea of starting a family. He was a free spirit and a bad boy musician, so Mom thought his reaction meant he was serious about her.

"Dusty followed him to some ranch in Northern California where he said he had family. It turned out to be a bunch of people living in teepees in some remote mountain campground. It wasn't clear how they were his "family." It was weird at first, but everyone was nice and they took care of her. He had a way of explaining everything in a way that made her feel like she was the crazy one.

"But then slowly, she started to realize he was giving orders to everyone at the campground and that he was sleeping with a bunch of the other women.

"When she confronted him, he somehow convinced her it was her fault she was upset about him sleeping around. He was, or is, a master manipulator.

"After I was born, it was clear to her that he wasn't going to legally marry her. He would travel for gigs and bring back more women. She knew she needed a plan to get out. She was also smart, and she found out where the group stashed all their cash. She started squirreling money away a little at a time and buried it.

"I look at the strong woman who raised me now, and I can't believe everything she put up with. When I was about seven years old, the DEA raided the camp—because they were dealing in drugs, guns, you name it. If it was on the black market, they were into it. and Mom took this as her chance to get away. She grabbed as much cash as she could fit in her backpack and we headed down the mountain. It was scary. It rained, and she ended up carrying me on her back for some of the trek. But we made it.

"And then she moved us to Southern California to start her life over. We've been in Sea Grove ever since. She saw that this old record store was for sale, so she used her stash of cash to buy the whole damn building.

"It's never been a gold mine. Mom's got a kind heart and is always giving her money and products away, but it keeps her busy and helps her to have something to do than feel guilty about stealing all that money."

Zara's chair had somehow moved right up against Kai's by the time Zara was finished telling her story. She was surprised to find she didn't feel alarmed in the slightest to find that Kai's arms were around her waist. She felt honored and protected. She kind of wanted to stay just like this, his tanned, beefy arms making her feel safe from all the stupidity of the world.

"Hey," he said. "Thank you for telling me your story."

Chapter 10

K *ai*

HIS LIPS WERE SO close to hers he could feel the heat coming off her. He could feel her breath rising and falling as he held her close. As she told her story, he had dared to put his arms around her. He had to do something, and it was the best thing he could think to do.

She might hold on to a cold persona, but she needed someone to be close to her. He felt unbelievably happy that she let him be a part of her space.

Her scent beckoned him to push even further. They were so close he guessed she could feel his heart racing. He stole a downward glance, where her tattered Ramones tee-shirt was torn into a deep vee, revealing her cleavage that could only be seen from this angle, close up. The sight of the tops of her breasts made his cock spring to life but also triggered the protective nature in him. He didn't want anyone else to look at her cleavage like that, or to have the reaction he was having.

Kai considered himself a very enlightened man. Never shamed a female for dressing as revealing as she wanted to. But the inner caveman in him sent a message that her breasts were for his eyes only. His mouth. His hands.

He waited for a signal. And then he got it. She darted her eyes down to his mouth and licked her lips.

The next moment, the bar, the cheap candles, the music, and the whole world of their broken pasts fell away like dry husks. What was left was a new, soft, fresh thing. It was only them. Together. *Us.*

Her soft lips yielded to his and filled his senses like warm salted caramel. His hand went to her jawline as he deepened the kiss. Kai could not wait to explore her mouth. He was about to try tasting her lips with his tongue when suddenly, they were interrupted.

"Kai, you're on!"

The sound came from the stage there karaoke deejay was announcing his name over the loudspeaker.

Well, shit.

Chapter 11

Z _ara_
"Yours was the first face I saw;
I think I was blind before I met you."

If someone had told Zara she would fall flat-on-her-face in love with a guy over a song, she might believe it. If that someone told her the moment would be at karaoke, and the song would be "The First Day of My Life," by Bright Eyes, she would have thought it was just too perfectly sappy. She had actually pictured a scenario closer to being brought up on stage during a Dropkick Murphys concert and being proposed to by…any of the members.

But, again, Kai turned all her notions upside down.

All she could tell you was the way he sang that sweet song to her wasn't one bit sappy. Perhaps it was the way his eyes kept drifting down to her breasts. He was letting her know what he thought with his words, but his eyes were telling her exactly what he wanted to do with her.

Would she let him? Probably.

Did she want to walk through the gauntlet of having to sing in public to get there? Not really.

Did she need to tell him she was a virgin? That might be a good idea.

When the song ended, Kai hopped down off the stage. "Your turn, beautiful," he said with a swagger and a wink.

"We could just get out of here and finish that kiss," she tried.

A look of smoldering hunger shadowed his face. He wolfed down his beer and slammed the bottle on the table. "Here's what's going to happen. You're going to sing a song. And then I'm going to watch you sing. And then I'll know."

"You'll know what?"

"Whether or not we're going to end up together."

Zara was confused. "Didn't I just tell you I wanted to finish that kiss? You're pretty much guaranteed a hookup with me tonight."

"That's not what I meant. I meant, whether or not I'm going to marry you."

Zara knew this kind of talk should send her running to the hills. "Marry?"

You don't bring that up on a first date. Relationship suicide, right? But…somehow the idea wasn't scaring her. Why wasn't it scaring her? It definitely should be. Her cautious side was telling her to leave right now. But the other side, the side that belonged to her heart, told her not to overreact.

The audience got tired of waiting for Zara to decide, and someone else hopped up and started in with "Faith" by George Michael. Kai took his seat next to Zara and she inhaled deeply his masculine scent.

She allowed herself to feel good when he was close.

"You can tell all that by watching me sing?"

"I can tell a lot of things by watching a person sing. And then after that, I'll take you home, where I will either sleep on the sofa or make you come with my mouth. The choice is up to you."

"Who the fuck do you think you are?" she said, finishing her seltzer, trying not to let her voice shake at the shock of him bringing up the proposition of oral sex.

"I think you know. And with your mother being out of town, there's no way I'm letting you sleep in that apartment alone."

"I'm a grown-ass woman."

"Then get your grown ass on the stage."

IT ONLY TOOK a few seconds to decide, but it felt like an agonizing hour. She had put less thought into which Ivy League school she should go to. This should be an easy choice.

Finally, she stood up and mounted the stairs to the stage and whispered something to the deejay.

She took the mic and waited for the opening chords of "The Tide is High" by Blondie.

Fortunately, it was a short song, but she felt like she was on stage for an eternity. She was that damn horny. The thought of having his arms around her again was too much. It was making her hands shake, and as a result, she nearly dropped the microphone twice.

But then, halfway through, she found Kai's eyes. He was trained on her like a wolf, and she was his hypnotized prey. His gaze on her as she sang made her feel like they were the only two people in the room. He was protecting her even while she was up on stage, and he wasn't going to stand for anybody to boo her.

"The tide is high and I'm holding on. I'm gonna be your number one."

She channeled her inner Debbie Harry and soldiered through. She even threw in a little hip sway and the audience cheered. He was right. This was fun.

Kai flashed her a huge smile, which then caused her to smile, and the audience was 100 percent on her side. Sure, they were all drunk as skunks, but still. She finally got the message. If she looked like she was having a good time, they would enjoy watching her. And they seemed to like her. In fact, they started singing along.

When the song was over, she felt like she was at the top of a mountain. It was ridiculous to feel this way in a divey noodle house on a Tuesday night, but she did. Zara took a bow and waved to the crowd, who cheered loudly. Some drunk woman even whistled.

She noticed Kai was standing and clapping, looking at her intensely. He held out a hand to help her off the stage, but she had a surprise for him. She'd always wanted to jump into someone's arms and be carried off, *Officer and a Gentleman* style.

"Get ready," she said to him, and leaped.

Chapter 12

K *ai*

AS KAI WATCHED Zara sing that silly song that he couldn't help but love, he was ready to pounce on the stage and take her right there in front of everyone.

He could see she was nervous, so he trained his eyes on her. It didn't take long for her to loosen up and start to sway her hips from side to side. With one sexy sway, she went from stomp-the-shit-out-of-your-heart intimidating to I-dare-you-to-take-your-eyes-off-my-body. He surely would not. Not for the rest of his natural born life if he could help it. When the audience cheered her sexy little moves, she upped her game and put some stank on it. Kai growled possessively. Who would have guessed what was hiding underneath all those black clothes?

Kai licked his lips as he watched her. This song was interminably long. But she was having fun. And holy shit…

she could sing! She had a really, really good voice. Kind of sweet and simple but with a little bit of and edge of Stevie Nicks.

This was giving Kai a really good idea. Someday they would be singing together.

When the song ended, he wanted to get out of there as soon as possible. He stood and held out his hand to help her down the stairs. But to his surprise, she stage-dived into his arms.

Kai was ready for anything when it came to Zara and snatched her out of the air and into his waiting arms as the crowd cheered.

As he stomped through the bar and out into the street, she hugged his neck and said into his ear, "Thank you, that was fun."

He laughed and replied, "Babe, you don't know what fun is. We're about to have a lot more of it."

BEAUTIFUL ZARA HAD his heart from the first time she'd nearly scared the piss out of him. The moment she had spun around and stared him down, he knew what he wanted to do with his life, and at the same time, knew he was going to have to step up his game to get what he wanted.

Listening to her story made him want her all the more, to protect her and show her that he could be trusted, and that he would never allow anyone to treat her or her mother that way again. Seeing her on stage clinched it. He needed her in his life. Forever. Now he just needed to figure out how to tell her the worst of it.

He carried her down the street, all the way back to

Beach Avenue and up to her flat, where he tossed her onto her bed with enthusiasm.

"You are amazing, Zara."

She reached up and touched his face, trailing down his throat, her hands wandering over his chest, resting on the waistband of his jeans. "People say a lot of things. I'm scary. I'm organized. I'm smart. I'm intimidating. I'm Wednesday Addams at summer camp. But never 'amazing.'"

Kai hovered over top of her, cradling her head and kissing her face all over. "You *are* amazing…and beautiful…and kind…and interesting…and funny…and sexy as fuck…and you are in my head like nobody else on this earth."

Zara smiled and bit her lip as Kai kissed her cheeks, her forehead, her nose, her neck. "Well, there's one other detail you should be aware of. I'm a virgin."

He traced kisses over her collarbone, thinking he needed this shirt of hers gone as soon as possible.

"Did you hear what I said?"

"Yeah," he said roughly. "So? We all have secrets."

She seemed surprised. "'So'? I thought it would be kind of a big deal."

He chuckled and smoothed her hair back. He could run his fingers through her silken dark locks all day every day. It felt like water cascading over his skin. "It's only a big deal because of the coincidence," he said, stroking her neck and running his finger down over the neckline of her shirt.

"What coincidence? You're not a virgin," she said, eyeing him suspiciously.

"What is a virgin?" Kai replied. "Virginity is an illusion. It's just a label."

As he spoke, he could feel her breasts touching him with every inhale.

"It carries a lot of weight for me," Zara said. "It's hard to let myself go."

Kai smiled and then claimed her mouth with his. She opened up to him and welcomed his tongue. She had roiling passions beneath that cool exterior. He could stay here like this and kiss her forever. But he still sensed a certain nervousness.

"Maybe it'll help you feel less vulnerable if I take my clothes off first?"

She bit her sexy, pouty lip and said, "I've been wondering about that bare chest all week."

The thought of her staring at his body like a piece of meat made Kai feel even hornier.

He pulled off his shirt over his head, and the way she looked at his chest, his abs, his arms, his shoulders, was like a cat eyeing a tetra fish in an aquarium. She looked as if she she was thinking of all manner of evil things. He felt totally objectified. And he liked it.

No, he loved it.

She was trembling and licked her lips. He dropped his jeans and drawers in the next hot second.

Zara's face turned red, but he sensed it was not out of embarrassment but out of pure excitement and antic-ipation.

"You're naked," she said with a shy grin.

"I am."

Her eyes fell to his rock-hard cock. Feeling her gaze on his manhood kicked his need up a notch. "It's big," she added, her eyes widening.

"I'll be gentle," he replied.

"I'm not worried about that, I know you will. I'm fasci-nated. I've never seen one before…in person."

Kai was ecstatic that he was her first. And she would be the first to put her hands on him.

He approached the bed where she was propped up on her side, admiring him like Cleopatra and a manservant. "Touch it," he said.

Zara sat up and gingerly held him in her hands. Kai was over the moon with the sensation of her hands on his cock. She stroked and explored until he was about to burst with lust for her.

Then she surprised him by opening her mouth and kissing the tip.

"Oh god," he said, sharply inhaling, feeling a bead of pre-cum forming on the tip. "Not yet."

She backed off in surprise. In the next second, he had her on her back and was spreading her legs apart.

"First I get you ready for me."

"But I want to…"

"Not yet. First, this…"

With that, he had her skirt hiked up and fishnets ripped away. Her lacy panties he pulled to the side and found her heat with his mouth.

"Oh fuck!" she gasped.

Her folds were soaked for him, and the thought of that doused him with the deepest joy.

He devoured her sticky center like a bear at the honey jar. Her flesh was ripe berries in the heat of summer, waiting to be picked.

Her moans grew with intensity. "Holy shit, that's nice."

He teased, licked and gorged himself on her pussy. She rocked her hips upward toward him, urging him to make himself at home. He found her clit and flicked it with his tongue, the resulting moans and trembles from her making him ache to be inside her that much more.

Her body started to tense with the coming orgasm. He

backed off of her clit and sank his tongue into her, tasting her depth, which was fully ripe just for him.

"I want to find that last barrier to you before I break it."

She sighed as Kai snaked one arm up underneath her shirt and took hold of her breast while his other hand massaged the inside of her upper thigh. His tongue explored deeper, his face soaking in her sweet juices, and found her ripe little cherry. He backed off then, inserting his finger to massage that spot to prepare her for him.

Zara writhed under him in pleasure. As his finger explored her hymen, his tongue once again found her clit and teased it into submission.

"Kai, I feel like something strange is happening," she said, gasping for air.

"Does it feel good?"

"Everything feels good. More than good."

"It means you're about to come. All over my face, baby."

She fell off a cliff and let herself go into a full-body spasm. Her back arched as her sex gripped his finger and she fell apart, crying his name.

He kept working over her clit, extending her climax.

"Kai! Oh my god," she moaned.

In the midst of her pleasure, Kai pulled himself up on his forearms, hovering over her again.

"I want to watch your face while you come," he said.

Her hands gripped his shoulders, her nails digging in with exquisite pain.

Her whole body responded to the pleasure he gave her. Her face was free of sarcasm.

He smiled.

"What?" she said weakly.

"I finally wiped that sarcastic sneer off your face," he said.

She breathed, "You love it."

"I love you."

Her eyes grew wide, and she wrapped her legs around him. "I'm ready."

Kai lifted her shirt and pulled down her bra, admiring her sweet, flushed breasts. He sucked gently on one nipple and teased the other with his thumb. She had the sweetest little body he'd ever seen, and it was ten times sweeter touching it underneath her clothes.

He tugged her panties off completely and placed just the tip of his cock at her entrance. She responded by wrapped her legs around his waist and drawing him in closer.

"Wait," he said. "Take your time."

"I don't want to take my time. I want you all the way in me."

"Let me get protection…"

But she was not having it. Her legs squeezed, and damn if he didn't let her. He knew he should stop her. He had a responsibility to protect her, but at the same time… Damn.

He allowed her to pull him in and he didn't stop. Could not stop. He felt her cherry at the tip of his cock and knew she was ready. He pushed against it and felt it break.

She sucked in her breath. He waited to make another move. Her forehead furrowed for the slightest second, but then she said, "It's good. Keep going."

He pushed in further, and deeper, and her body around his was warm and tight and still soaking wet.

He was so happy he had waited to do this particular thing with her and only her. They fit each other perfectly.

He rode her, lights on, eyes on each other and their hearts open. The perfection of their bodies together carried him away until it was too late to pull out. He released inside her with a roar of pleasure that nearly blinded him with relief and ecstasy.

"Zara, I ..." He tried to apologize when he realized he'd just released a spectacular amount of cum inside her.

But she was in another place entirely.

As their matched rhythm slowed down, she owned his mouth with hers; she owned his body with her hands. Everything about her had brought him to heel. She was perfection. She was his temptress. It didn't matter if she got pregnant, because he was never leaving her side.

Chapter 13

Z *ara*

ZARA WOKE up the next morning feeling…different than she expected.

More comfortable in her own skin.

She had expected to feel some sort of regret at not having used protection.

She expected to feel ten years older, with the associated concerns of a mature woman—as if having sex suddenly made a person have the urge to check her credit report and apply for a mortgage. She felt none of that.

Instead, she felt like she'd come home.

Like she'd given something up only to find the missing piece.

Kai was stroking her hair when she opened her eyes. "Hey, I need to talk to you about something."

"Uh-oh. Are you an alien? Are you married? You have a girlfriend waiting for you at the next Phish concert in Monterrey?"

"No," he chuckled. "I have to tell you that … some other shit went down in Oregon that I'm not ready to talk about. But I will. At some point."

Zara smiled. "The only thing I'm worried about is getting pregnant before I've even started getting my life started. And you don't have to worry about that because I've been on the pill since I was 17 to regulate my period. So, no worries. The only protection I'm worried about is my brain. I don't want to end up being gaslit and living in a teepee."

"What's wrong with a teepee?"

She punched him on his massive shoulder and he winced, jokingly.

"Nothing, if you're of a certain indigenous background. But don't you think it's a little inappropriate for other people to appropriate this as a cool, countercultural type of housing when their ancestors nearly decimated the cultures in which teepees came from?"

Kai sat up on his elbows and mulled it over for a minute. "I never thought of it that way, Ivy League, but you're absolutely right."

She shrugged. "I just read a lot. I wrote a thesis on cultural appropriation and the economic impact of it on indigenous cultures. I guess I wanted to find a way to ream my father without being able to tell him to his face that he's an asshole."

Kai rolled over on top of her. "Woman, talk to me more about economics, it gets me so fuckin' hard."

She smiled and opened her legs to him. Swiftly, Kai sat up cross-legged and pulled Zara onto his lap; she gasped in surprise at being in this new position. She blushed, but at the same time looked at him with a wicked fire in her eyes. "Oh really? Wait until I tell you about why trickle-down economics does not work."

Chapter 14

K*ai*

"OH, I don't know, I can feel your trickle-down working. You're wet for me again, aren't you, my lovely Zara?"

Without another word he lifted her hips and drew her downward, taking in the full length of him. Kai found he especially enjoyed this position with her; it allowed him to bury his face in her hair, cradle her entire body in his arms. Not to mention the kissing. Her lips, the taste of her mouth, was like nothing else on this earth. Everything felt heightened with her riding him, eye to eye. There was no tomorrow, no past. Only the present.

"Holy shit."

"Yes, baby girl. Tell me what you want."

"My whole body feels warm. You make me feel like I might burst into flames."

"And I'm here to write your name in the sky with that

fire." He cupped her ass with both hands, bringing her in as close to him as physics would allow. She arched her back, teasing his mouth with her round, perfect breasts in his face.

"I love that you waited," Kai murmured between kissing her breasts. "I love that I'm the only one who's ever been between your legs."

"I'm so glad you were the first to make me come."

"Hold on tight, princess, it's about to happen again."

Kai covered one nipple with his mouth and sucked, massaged and gently scraped with his teeth. Zara sucked in her breath. He let go of one of her ass cheeks and roughly grabbed hold of her other breast. She thrust against him in rhythm, and on the downbeat he gently squeezed and suckled her nipples a little harder. Each thrust was a step closer to heaven; each touch, noise, kiss and bite cut through all the bullshit and horrors of life on earth. He was Major Tom and he could almost see the stars.

Without warning, Zara's body seized in a sudden explosion of pleasure.

"Fucking hell!"

Her pussy pulsed around his cock, milking him dry once again. When she closed her eyes to let the climax wash over her with a magnificent shudder, he gazed up at her face. He could write a thousand songs about that face and never get it quite right.

She caught her breath as she trembled in his arms.

"That was…"

He claimed her mouth with a deep kiss while his hands wound through her hair.

"I ain't done, baby girl. I have plans for you later today."

Chapter 15

Z *ara*

THE RECORD SHOP was fairly dead that morning, and Zara didn't much feel like sorting through Dusty's receipts.

In fact, she didn't feel like doing any of her usual responsible tasks. She was feeling quite the opposite.

The only appealing thing to her was sitting in her mom's cushy armchair in the listening corner, where she could sit with her legs tucked under her and stare dreamily out the front window at the back of Kai's head. She didn't feel like having coffee, eating, or doing anything besides staring, with a stupid smile on her face.

She was just about to drift off to the sea breeze that wafted in through the propped open door while listening to Kai play "Ripple" by the Grateful Dead. She didn't know what it was about, but there were words about sunshine and water and cups being full and it seemed to match how she felt.

It was a good thing Dusty wasn't here. She'd be pumping Zara for details.

And then the flowers came; a delivery of a dozen dark purple tulips.

"These were the closest flowers I could find to black," Kai said when she stepped outside to thank him.

He set down his guitar in its case and towered over her, putting his arms around her bottom and lifted her up off her feet to plant on her a sweet, deep, long, passionate kiss.

"Get a room!" some passerby shouted good-naturedly.

Zara swooned so hard, she could feel her panties nearly going up in flames.

Kai laughed, "Perhaps this is the kind of kiss that belongs indoors."

"Screw it," she replied. "It's summertime and I'm in love."

Kai growled and lifted Zara up so she was sitting on the window sill. He planted himself between her legs and pressed against her, his back to the street. He wanted her to feel the rock hard need she was building inside his woven hemp shorts.

When Kai finally came up for air, she murmured and stroked his two-tone blond locks. "Thank you for last night."

He replied, "I want you to know I meant what I said. I. Love. You."

Everything turned to jello.

And then she realized what an idiot she was.

"Oh my god. I can't believe I didn't say it back. Well, not officially. I love you too."

"I know. Get inside and get your ass into the listening booth."

She looked at him sideways. "Why?"

"Just do it, woman."

"OK, but at least let me shut the door. That way we can hear if a customer comes."

Chapter 16

K *ai*

INSIDE THE LISTENING BOOTH, lined with heavy curtains to help block out outside sounds, Kai put a record on the turntable. He then turned to Zara and put a set of large, old-school headphones over her ears.

"What are you doing?"

He didn't answer, but pulled her close. He could Prince singing about the girl in the raspberry beret. He lifted Zara's top, stretching her lacy black bra to one side to reveal one breast. He claimed it for himself. It did, after all, belong to him now. He did the same with the other breast, as Zara gasped, her chest, neck and face blooming red for him.

"You're insatiable," she said, her eyes closed, lips parted.

"I could make you come like this. Right here. Right now."

"I wouldn't mind if you wanted to try."

His mouth owned her, his tongue swirled, his thumbs teased, his teeth grazed. All of it combined made Zara squirm.

"Kai, I want to touch you," she whispered, biting her lip. "I want you to feel what I'm feeling."

"Later," he growled against her chest. Instead, he teased and squeezed until she was almost out of breath.

He kept it up until she let out a knee-buckling orgasm. He caught her up in his arms and spread soft kisses across her chest, up her neck and down her jawline.

Just at that moment, the front doorbell rang out the cutesy version of the Ozzy tune.

"Customers," she gasped.

Kai helped straighten her mussed hair as she adjusted her bra and shirt to cover her breasts once again. He growled at seeing her perfect tits disappear. Hopefully she could make this annoying customer disappear and they could get back to business.

Kai followed Zara out of the listening booth. He was about to fade into the background, but then he caught the look on Zara's face.

She was staring at the customer who just walked in.

Her bottom lip started to tremble.

"Dad?"

Whoa.

Chapter 17

Z *ara*

THE LARGE, gray-haired man gestured to Kai. "Who the fuck is that?"

"Walter, what are you doing here?"

Kai took a step forward and instantly had his arm protectively around Zara.

She had not seen her biological father since she was seven years old, and now here he was.

"I go by 'Dad,' thank you very much."

Zara shook her head. "I barely know you. A dad is not someone who cheats and controls women. Who isolates a woman from her family. What is it you want?"

"Just got out on parole and wanted to say hello. Dusty here?"

She narrowed her eyes at him. "I don't have to give you any information."

Walter huffed. "I suppose she's not here, or else you wouldn't be slutting it up in here with this pothead."

"Sir, you need to watch what you say," Kai said, his voice calm but full of warning.

"Who the fuck are you?"

"Walter, this is Kai," Zara said.

"Kai what?"

That's when Zara realized she couldn't remember his last name from his driver's license. She felt like such an idiot.

She opened her mouth to speak, then glanced over at Kai.

"It's none of your business," she said.

"Stormcloud," Kai said.

Walter and Kai stood like columns and stared each other down. Zara needed to de-escalated the situation.

"OK. Walter, I'll tell Mom you stopped by. Is there a message I can leave with her?"

Walter didn't answer but kept staring at Kai.

"I'll wait," he said.

"She's not coming back today. She might not be back for a while."

"Oh, did she abandon you, too?"

Kai took a step forward. "Sir, it's time for you to leave."

"I don't think so. Seeing as old Dusty's got something that belongs to me."

"What the fuck are you talking about?"

"Come on, Zara, don't be naïve. You know she stole my money to move here and live her fancy life. My money and … well, some other shit that you don't need to know about. I had a private investigator track her down," Walter said.

Zara laughed bitterly. "Some P.I. Took him what, 13 years to find us?"

"I hired him last week when I got out of jail."

"Leave now, and maybe I'll be nice and not slap you with a protection order." she said.

Walter looked as if he were considering his options. "Fine. I'll be back. But tell that bitch I want my money and that memorabilia she took, and I'll leave the both of you alone."

Zara was incredulous. "What memorabilia?"

Walter scoffed. "Hell no. You think I'm gonna tell you so you can go and hide it? I wager your about as crafty as your old thief of a mother."

Chapter 18

K *ai*

NORMALLY A PEACE-LOVING FELLOW, Kai felt nothing but white hot rage at this asshole.

He knew his type. Unpredictable. Dangerous. Conniving.

The look on Walter's face, the tone in his voice gave Kai the feeling that he was amped up and ready to cause mayhem.

He reminded him of Bob.

Bob was the whole reason Kai had to leave Oregon.

And he wasn't about to let that trauma get the best of him. He had to stay calm.

When Walter finally left, he turned to Zara. "Babe. Don't worry. I got this. He is not going to even come in the door or speak to you or even look at you if you don't want him to. That's my promise."

She smiled up at him with those red lips and kohl-painted eyes. "You're such the boy scout."

"Don't even joke, Zara. I don't trust that guy. First blush, he's no good. Sorry to say that to you about your biological father, but…"

Zara scoffed. "Oh, please. He's a piece of shit."

Her words echoed his thoughts. But he had a hunch she wasn't spilling everything. "What's going on in your head?" he asked.

She smiled. "Nothing. I'm fine. Just seeing him again kicked up a lot of muck that has been dormant for a while, you know?"

Kai growled and wrapped her in a big bear hug.

Was it time to tell her the whole truth?

"Babe," he started. "I …"

"What is it?" she asked.

"…I just want you to know I'll be here for you, no matter what. I don't want you to worry. OK?"

She smiled. "I do trust you. Don't get all emo on me now, I can't be with a tortured soul."

He winked and wrapped her back up into another hug; their lips found each other and erased all the bad energy that remained.

Chapter 19

Z *ara*

HER CALL WENT RIGHT to her mother's voicemail. Again. "Mom, me again. I'm OK. I just miss you. Juice up your phone please, before I put out a missing person's report. And FYI, Walter's here. Well, not here. But he's in Sea Grove. Yeah. So there's that. Anyway, I guess I'll try calling Marti later to track you down. Love you."

Dusty was known to let her smartphone sit around without any juice in it on the regular. Zara sighed and set her phone down on the night-table. It was probably too early for Dusty to be awake anyway.

It had been a day since Walter had shown up, but Zara was trying not to let her guard down. Maybe he'd given up and crawled back under whatever rock he'd come out of. That would be nice.

Zara chose to focus on the moment. And in this

current moment, it was Monday. Vinyl Vixen was closed, along with many other businesses on Beach Avenue, as was the tradition.

She was planning on spending the whole day in bed, sleeping, having coffee, working on her secret project (making business cards for Kai, just in case anyone with clout happened to listen to his music and liked it) and then exploring all as-yet-unexplored sexual positions with Mr. Insatiable.

Maybe they could head up to Monterrey and pick up a copy of the Kama Sutra at a used book store.

She woke to a tickling sensation on the inside of her upper thigh. She sighed.

When Kai spoke, the sensation of his voice sent vibrations and tingles all through her most sensitive place. Her skin rejoiced every time his lips were near.

"Babe, I made coffee."

"Hmmm. My favorite four words."

"And then," Kai said, " we're going to have a picnic on the beach. Maybe a bonfire later on. Lots of making out."

She grinned. "OK, but when do we get to go back to bed and have more of the yummy sex?"

He nipped at her inner thigh with his teeth. "I thought that was what was happening right now?"

They never made it to that picnic or the bonfire. Instead, they spent the day devouring each other and keeping each other warm in her bed.

Zara appreciated all the ways in which Kai refused to leave her side. But honestly, didn't he need time to himself to tackle all of the projects around the building that he had promised to do for Dusty?

When Kai finally fell asleep again late that afternoon, spent, satisfied and snoring, Zara slipped out. She was starving and needed some sustenance.

Along the way down Beach Avenue, she inhaled the salty air and called Dusty again.

Voicemail. Again.

Everything along Beach Avenue was closed, so she ventured farther than she should have, to the fancy new gas station convenience store close to Highway 1, where you can order food made to order right from a touch screen. She ordered some tacos, burritos and about five other things that were sure to put her and Kai into a food coma. After she placed her order, her eyes fell on the dining area that advertised "free wifi." There sat a black-haired fellow in the corner booth.

Walter. *Shit.*

"Funny you should stop in," Walter said with a sneer as he stood and walked toward her, a little too quickly for her comfort.

"What are you doing here? Aren't you supposed to be working on a Monday afternoon. Like, isn't employment a condition of your parole? I'm just guessing."

Walter shrugged off her questions. "That guy is a fraud. That boyfriend of yours? He's a murderer."

Zara reared back. "What the fuck, Walter. Are you high or drunk?"

"I'm only high on life because I did my time and I'm a free man. Your man, on the other hand, has never paid his debt to society."

"You're insane."

"Am I? My P.I. friend and I have been digging up the dirt and your boyfriend shot a guy in Oregon. And then he just left the state. Did he tell you all of that?"

Zara had to work to keep her chin from quivering. But she'd be damned if this imbecile was going to make her cry. "Oh that guy? Yes. Of course I knew all that. Now get out of my face before I call your parole officer."

Before she grabbed her food and stalked out, Walter hissed, "Say hi to your mom for me. Tell her to give me a call. I can wait as long as I have to."

ZARA WALKED BACK up the street in a daze. She didn't know where to go or who to talk to. Fortunately, the phone rang and determined the rest for her.

"Mom? What's going on?"

"Oh baby, I'm on my way home right now. You got distracted on your last voicemail; you forgot to hang up the phone and I heard everything. I heard what Walter said. Listen. I am so sorry. I knew Walter was getting out of jail soon but I didn't think it was, like, yesterday. And I really didn't think he could find us so fast. I just got ... so distracted ... up here at Galen and Marti's."

"And what have you been doing while I've been getting harassed by the village idiot?" Zara's tone was reaching beyond sarcastic and bordering on nasty. She did not care. She was pissed.

"Zara, honey, I went to Santa Barbara to hide something that I took when you and I left him."

"Ma, I don't want to talk about any of that. Why am I hearing that Kai shot some guy in Oregon?

Dusty moved along. "I'm on my way home and we can talk in person."

Zara could not believe it. Her mother didn't even seem shocked. She also wasn't denying the accusation of Kai shooting somebody.

"Ma, tell me what the fuck is going on?"

Dusty sighed. "OK. A few days before you came home from school, Kai showed up looking for a place to perform his music, and we got to talking. I found out he shot his uncle. It was very sad. But he was protecting his aunt. He caught him hitting her. Kai was working for a private security company in the neighborhood. He told me the whole story. I guess … I assumed he would have told you by now. But I checked out his story and it was all true. So I knew if Walter showed up, he could protect us. I asked him to keep an eye on the shop and on you while I was gone."

Zara could not believe what she was hearing. Had everyone been lying to her for the last two weeks?

It was time to go for a walk and think about things.

Chapter 20

K *ai*

YOU READY TO TELL ME *the truth about Portland?*

Shit. It wasn't as if Kai wasn't going to tell her the whole story. He was waiting for the right time. What the hell was going on? The memories suddenly came flooding back and clouded his thoughts before he could think through how to respond to Zara.

THE PATROL CAR'S *flashing lightbars reflected in the damp pavement. The blood. The screams. The fists. It was all over now.*

He had brought murder to this quiet, gated retirement village.

But that asshole uncle of his would never lay a hand on Aunt Jo again. Kai had made sure of it.

True, Kai never should have been the one to respond to the situa-

tion at that address he heard over the police scanner. He knew he should let the police handle it and stay in the security gatehouse, where he worked nights.

He had known going in exactly what was happening. Bob was using his fists to get his point across.

Kai turned off his security radio to silence his colleagues' warnings against him going there.

When he arrived, he parked his car to block the end of the driveway in case Bob decided to drive off.

Kai slammed his car door shut and approached the front door. He didn't even knock. Proper protocol was out the window.

He bolted toward the sound of angry voices, and entered the kitchen, gun drawn.

It was over before Bob could hurt her again. No more of her resisting pressing charges. No more court orders that don't work.

In the end, the police investigation cleared him of any charges. But using a gun to kill a bad guy — a real life human being — is not what it's like in the movies.

It changed him.

The security company let him go. He went to counseling.

Kai spent months putting his life back together, taking odd jobs here and there. Working his ass off to take care of Aunt Jo, now that she'd lost her husband and the second income he had provided for her.

But she pushed him to leave town and find himself.

"You need a change of scenery," she said. "This place has too many bad memories. Go somewhere sunny. Follow your heart. Play your music and find your happy."

"My home is here with you," he had protested.

Aunt Jo smiled. "Go be in the sun with people your own age, and don't come back without some babies for me to squeeze."

KAI HAD THOUGHT he'd found his happy in Zara. And now she was likely to kick his ass all over Beach Avenue for not telling her the entire truth.

Or worse. She might dump his ass. Kai preferred the first option. He certainly deserved the ass kicking.

Kai hated communicating over text. He punched in the reply:

Come back to me. Let's talk about it.

Instead of kicking his ass or dumping his ass, she somehow delivered the worst option of all.

Before you and I go any further, I need some time to take care of some things.

That meant the dreaded word "space." She wanted "space." Kai had not even thought of that being a possibility.

Space is limbo. Torture. Unacceptable.

Fuck this.

He stomped down to the record shop on the off chance that Zara might be there. But, of course she wasn't.

Well, he thought, *she can't give me space. She has to come back to work, and I'm not going anywhere.*

Chapter 21

K *ai*

SWEAT POURED INTO HIS EYES. Having long, thick hair was tough in the summer for a guy who was handy. He was now seeing the value of those 1980s workout headbands and was seriously considering bringing them back into fashion.

Allowing Zara to have space was unacceptable to this newfound possessiveness he was experiencing. She belonged to him. They belonged together.

But with Zara, he could not simply claim what was his. He had to convince her they belonged together, without her realizing that's what he was doing.

Hence, replacing the entire ceiling of the shop without allowing a single bit of dust to fall on a customer's head in the process. He worked around the shop at night; during the day, he busked out front and kept an eye on her without crowding her. He slept little.

Dusty had come home and tried talking some sense into Zara, but it all fell on deaf ears.

And now with so much time on his hands, not only did Kai have the entire Fourth of July block party completely planned, he had also completed a shit ton of work around the building. He had installed a security system for the shop and for the flat; built a stage for the block party; hired security for the event; fixed the store's wonky sound system; and applied fresh coats of paint in the restrooms.

If Kai he couldn't fill his time with Zara, he had to at least be useful.

Today, his goal was to fix the water leak in the shop. He had removed all of the ugly drop-ceiling material—thank god for no asbestos—and was hammering away at the corroded seams in the water pipes.

After that, he decided, he would update the air conditioning vents. Then. he would paint all of the exposed duct work one uniform color to give height and interest to the room.

The hammering did little to work out his frustrations over Zara.

In the meantime, Dusty had returned to Vinyl Vixen.

Things were tense all around.

If Kai used his time to work extra hard around the shop, Zara was uncharacteristically unproductive. She showed up late to work. Kai watched her messing up the totals in the till at the end of the day. Zara wasn't herself.

One this day, as Zara slept in late, again, Dusty addressed the issue with Kai.

He kept working as she spoke.

"Kai, it wasn't me who told her. It was her father, Walter. He had some no-good friends of his do some digging on you, and he told her. I'm sorry it spooked her. But just hang in there."

Kai thanked her and got back to work on the pipes.

Any sane man would have cut and run. Made everyone more comfortable by leaving. Bow out. Let them have their peace.

But he was far from sane when it came to Zara.

For now, the old jailbird seemed to enjoy spending his probation time finding free Wi-Fi to leave terrible reviews of Vinyl Vixen on Yelp!, smearing them on Twitter and Facebook. No social media were safe from his attack campaign.

The piece of shit wasn't going to come near the shop while Kai was there, now that he knew what he was capable of.

Instead, Walter was trying to draw Dusty out.

Chapter 22

Z *ara*

BY THE TIME the Fourth of July arrived, Zara knew it was time to move on.

She had managed to keep her distance from Kai in order to get her head straight these past couple of weeks. But now, she was ready. She would have to tell Kai she had made up her mind, if he was ready to hear it.

Working together to set the stage for the party was torture. They kept bumping into each other, literally.

Finally, Dusty could not take the icy silence any longer and gave them the job of rounding up a list of decorations she needed. The list was a mile long and had them snaking all over town in Kai's Volkswagen bus.

"You know that Dusty doesn't need any of this shit on this list. She did this to us on purpose, to force us to talk. Her machinations know no bounds."

Kai offered, "Yeah, but is that such a bad thing?"

"It is when people aren't upfront about it. Why didn't she tell me the truth about you? And why didn't you?"

Kai pulled over to the side of the road and parked next to some rocks near a path that led to a beach access. "Did you ever stop to think that maybe people wait to tell you everything is because you can be a little…I don't know… stand-offish?"

"Excuse me?"

"Be honest. Would you have dated me if you had known from the beginning that I came down here to decompress after shooting my aunt's abusive husband?"

"Maybe. It's kind of badass, what you did."

Kai looked shocked. "I thought you were scared of me because of it."

She shook her head. "No. I was angry because you didn't tell me. And … I needed space so I could dig up dirt on my father. Turns out, he's in violation of his parole. I found out the name of his parole officer and we've been in contact. Cops are going to pick him up tonight at the Fourth of July party."

It was all true. In the days since she'd last been confronted by Walter, Zara had stayed under the radar to do her own dirty work. She had changed strategies and decided to pretend to warm up to Walter.

After she texted Kai about needing time to think, she circled back to the gas station.

Walter had looked surprised, maybe even annoyed, at first, to see her.

"Look," Zara tried, "Mom's in trouble. You and I know she's not great with money. But I am."

Walter had looked at her suspiciously at first, but then invited her to have a seat.

Over the next couple of weeks, they met in secret.

Always in public, but Zara made sure it was always far from Beach Avenue and anyone who knew her. It took some time, but she eventually convinced Walter to let her help him find what he wanted.

She had handed him the flier. "Come to the party. Mom will be busy. Kai will be helping mom. I can duck out and find what you're looking for. But you have to promise that when you sell that thing, you'll split it with mom and be on your way. Get your shit together. Leave her alone and we'll leave you alone. I won't even tell your parole officer where you are."

Walter had looked her up and down with a wary grin and considered his options.

Zara waited.

She hated to admit it to herself, but she and her dad had one thing in common. They never let go when they wanted something.

Finally, after what had felt like a millennia, Walter bought the plan. Hook. Line. Sinker.

Zara explained the whole situation, including the part where he would show up at the back alley behind Vinyl Vixen during the Fourth of July party. Zara would take him inside and the local cops would be waiting to take him back to jail on a warrant to extradite from Northern California.

He gritted his teeth. "I should never have been there that night. I should have let the police handle the call. And taking someone's life, even a bad guy, may look badass on paper. But it seriously fucking messed me up and I don't like to talk about it. I was going to tell you on my time. On my terms. Yes, you deserved to know that, but it is my story to tell. Not your dad's and not your mom's."

By the time he was done talking, Zara's tears streamed

down her cheeks. She opened the passenger door and stepped out. "Let's walk," she said.

"Why?"

She smiled through her tears. "Because I refuse to kiss and make up inside this ridiculous van."

Chapter 23

K *ai*

GRATEFUL THINGS WERE BACK on solid ground with Zara, Kai was singing and playing better than ever at the party that night.

People were dancing, drinking, having a blast.

His tip jar was completely full, and between songs, he had Zara count it out for him.

In just two hours, he'd made about $300. He announced to the crowd, "Thank you all for your tips. I just wanted to let you know I'll be donating all the tips I make tonight to the shelter. And thanks to all the tickets sold, after expenses we'll have raised $4,000."

Everyone clapped and cheered. Then Dusty took the stage and whispered something that totally blew Kai's mind. He handed her the mic so she could tell everyone the news.

"We have an update on that number. It seems we have an unexpected celebrity guest in our midst tonight, who has just informed me he's going to match whatever we raise. So far that's $8,000. Who here thinks we can top $10,000?"

Everyone cheered. Zara looked at Kai and mouthed the words, "Who is it?"

Kai shrugged and scanned the crowd. He didn't see anyone he recognized other than the locals.

Dusty finished talking and handed the mic back to Kai, who said, "Thanks, everyone. This next song is one that I wrote for a special woman who I've recently gotten to know. She's smart, fun, and despite her outward appearance, as kind and generous as they come. She's worked her ass off to make this party happen for you tonight. She's a good woman and I feel lucky to have her in my life."

You got eyes like Joan
You got lips like Debbie
You got a voice like Stevie
And a soul like Patti
Girl, you stomped the shit out of my heart
And I'm coming back for more.
You got heart like Chrissie
Fire like Janis
Legs like Tina
And the sweetness of Alanis
Yeah, you kicked the shit out of my heart.
And I'm coming back for more
Yeah, you stomped the bullshit right out
And I ain't never gonna close that door.

. . .

ZARA DISAPPEARED in the middle of the song. He supposed the time had come for Zara to carry out the plan to meet up with Walter at Vinyl Vixen.

He'd just have to play it for her later. She'd be ready for him to sing her to sleep, after what Kai was planning to do to her tonight.

As he sang, he smiled to himself at the thought of bending his woman over the bed while fireworks lit up the night sky outside his window.

In the next moment, he saw Dusty talking to an older fellow. Kai suddenly realized the older man was, in fact, the anonymous celebrity donor. She was talking and dancing and acting friendly and flirting with none other than Big Daddy. Jed. Big Daddy. Masters.

Holy Mary, Joseph, Baby Jesus, seven angels and a donkey.

It was as close to Kai would ever get to a religious experience. For him, this was seeing the pope.

Kai could not believe he was performing on stage right in front of that guy. It was all he could do to hold himself together enough to finish the song. He felt like a massive fraud in the presence of such greatness.

Keep it together and finish the song, dude.

When the song ended, he lost sight of Big Daddy. Kai excused himself for five minutes to get some water. As he descended from the stage, he nearly bumped right into his idol.

"Big Daddy!"

The silver-bearded hulk of a man held out his hand to shake Kai's. "I hate that nickname. Just call me Jed."

The man's voice was a deep baritone, but calming and disarming.

"Yes, sir. I mean, Jed. I…wow. I'm a huge, huge fan. This is such an honor."

"Well, I'm a big fan of Dusty, so you should be used to being around greatness."

Kai was confused. "Really?"

Jed continued, "I've been ordering rare vinyl from her for years and just recently had the chance to meet her. She told me about you, and I want to ask you about that song."

Kai could barely process what was happening right now. But the matter at hand was, he needed to find Zara. He had to make sure she was OK and that this cocka-mamie (but also badass) plan of hers didn't get her in trouble. He could not believe what he was about to say.

"I'm sorry, sir…Big Daddy…I mean Jed. I gotta go find my girl."

Jed's grip was firm and his eyes were warm. "I completely understand. Go find her, or else what's music even about, am I right?"

Kai nodded and took off.

Chapter 24

Zara

"HE SAID HE'D BE HERE," Zara said, checking the time on her phone, as the two sheriff's deputies watched and waited inside the closed record shop.

Walter was late.

And she was beginning to feel incredibly foolish.

She could hear the music and the carousing in the distance at the block party. A feeling started to creep in that she should have kept her mouth shut and minded her own business. Let the authorities deal with her father rather than try to manipulate him.

She looked at the deputies, who were checking their watches.

One of them suggested, "If you have an address where he's currently living, we can execute the warrant at his home in the morning."

Zara's stomach churned. "It's no use. He never told me where he was staying and I never asked. I've just been meeting with him at different places around town. Hell, he could be sleeping anywhere, like a vagrant."

"It's not unheard of," the other deputy said.

Just then, a call came over their radios. The dispatcher was calling for response to something happening out in the county.

The deputies looked at each other and then the first one said, "I'm sorry ma'am, but this call takes precedent over this type of warrant. Let us know where he's staying, when you find out, and we'll get him. We suggest you take out a protection order against him if he starts making physical threats and in the meantime, take a firearms class."

She said goodbye to the officers and saw them out to the side street where they had parked their unmarked patrol cars.

She mentally kicked herself as she headed back in to re-set the security system at Vinyl Vixen.

Chapter 25

K*ai*

AS SOON AS Kai rounded the corner to the side street, he had to keep himself from nearly going full Hulk.

And the reason he was so angry — no, enraged — was the sight of Walter, hiding behind trash cans in the alleyway.

Kai froze, backed himself into a nook at the back of the florist shop, and watched.

If the man was laying in wait behind the trash cans, things had not gone according to plan.

And the back door of the shop was wide open.

Which meant only one thing: Zara was in trouble.

But whatever shit Walter was planning, it was never going to land at Zara's feet.

Kai watched as Walter checked the alleyway entry points, and made his move.

When Walter approached the recessed doorway, his way in was blocked by a hulking blonde beast in a 1990s baja tunic.

"Hey buddy," Kai said in a pretend-friendly tone. "What you up to back here?"

Walter put his hands up, "I have some family business to attend to. So if you'll kindly step aside."

Kai threw his head back and laughed. "That's cute."

Walter looked at him warily. "That there's the laugh of a psychopath. Like I've been telling Zara."

Kai snatched the front of Walter's shirt. His voice rumbled. "Say her name again. I'm looking forward to head-butting you."

"Zara is my da-," he started, cut off by the crack of Kai's forehead against his.

Walter stumbled backward.

Kai stepped down from the doorway and approached Walter. "Turn around and leave Sea Grove now, and maybe you'll get to live the rest of your life in peace. Try to do the right thing."

Walter scoffed. "What does that mean? You won't try to turn me in to the authorities?"

Kai pointed at Walter's chest. "No. It means if you don't bother Zara or Dusty ever again, I won't fucking murder you."

Walter backed away slowly, matching Kai's gaze as he walked. Then he turned tail and ran like a little bitch.

Just then, Kai heard a female gasp.

Kai turned, and Zara stood there with her hand over her mouth.

"That was him. He was here? Now what?"

"He's gone. Don't worry. It's going to be OK."

She fell into his arms. "I had it all planned out. It was perfect. He needs to go back to jail.

"Eh, sooner or later someone will pick him up for larceny or just for being a jackass. That's a federal charge, right?"

She exhaled some of the tension that had been building up.

"Are you OK?" he asked, tracing his thumb over both of her cheekbones.

She nodded silently, still covering her mouth. Then she put her hand to Kai's forehead. "But are you OK?"

Kai smiled. "I'll have a goose egg but otherwise, I'm fine." He covered her hand with his own, and drew it to his lips.

She sighed. "Let's lock up and get back to the party. Mom's probably wondering where we got off to."

Chapter 26

Z *ara*

FROM BEHIND THE STAGE CURTAIN, Zara went over the words. Of course she knew it by heart. Who doesn't know the words to "I Can't Help Falling in Love with You"? Elvis was her private jam. Whenever she felt lonely or sad or sappy, Elvis always helped. And now she couldn't think of anything better than to sing in front of not just a bar full of people but a whole crowd of locals who had known her since she was just a seven-year-old chicken-legged squirt running around the beach.

As she was doing her deep breathing, suddenly she was met by a hallucination. Or at least, it had to be a hallucination. Big Daddy was standing in front of her. Yeah. That Big Daddy.

"Um…" she stammered. "Is this happening?"

"You must be Zara," the older gentleman said with a

smile that reached his devastatingly gorgeous, crinkled eyes.

"Holy fuck!" she blurted, and her anxiety spiked. "Oh my god. I mean…aren't you…?"

Big Daddy laughed. "Yes, it's me. Just Jed. Just another guy who appreciates music."

Zara's throat went dry and she squeaked, "That's about the biggest understatement of the century. No, millennium."

He smiled and then said, "Could you tell your fella I'd like to buy that song from him?"

Jeb could have knocked Zara over with a microscopic owl feather.

"I'll make it easy for you. I'm going on tour tomorrow. Just tell him to get my number from Dusty. Don't call my manager and definitely not my asshole publicist. Call me directly and I'll make sure he's well compensated."

Then Zara summoned her brain back into the moment and reached into her pocket. "Here," she said, handing Jeb the business cards that she'd just finished for Kai but as yet had not had the chance to show to him. "Even better, here's his card."

Jed took it and departed with a nod and a wink through the curtain. And Zara was left feeling like she'd just been visited by a benevolent ghost. Terrified, stunned and overjoyed.

"Well, I guess we know who the anonymous donor is now," she said aloud to herself.

When she took the stage, she picked up the mic. Kai was watching her, surprised.

"I know you think I'm stand-offish sometimes. Well, this is about as fuckin' vulnerable as it gets. Here goes."

She started singing.

Wise men say

Only fools rush in…

After the first three words, Kai backed her up with his guitar. Of course he knew the chords by heart.

Eventually, she settled into her voice and her confidence grew. People were starting to pair off and slow dance together. It made her happy to see it.

And, holy shit, there was her mother, dancing with Big Daddy. Could this day get any weirder? No. No, it could not.

Suddenly, she realized she was not singing a cappella anymore. She looked over to her left, where Kai was closing in on her to share the mic.

When the song ended the crowd went absolutely insane.

"I love you, Zara. But you gotta sing more."

Her sight blurred by tears, she cupped his face. "I promise."

Chapter 27

K *ai*

"ZARA LANE RHODES, I promise to love you, and I promise to never make you live in a teepee or follow a jam band around the country. OK, maybe two Phish concerts, tops."

Zara replied, "Make that one pint of Phish Food ice cream on the porch while you play their songs on your guitar."

Kai grinned. "And I promise to let you set your alarm to the Sex Pistols every morning."

"Deal," she said with a smirk.

The officiant, who was, of course, an ordained minister and Elvis impersonator (circa-*Jailhouse Rock*), announced, "I pronounce you husband and wife. You may kiss."

Kai took his bride's face in both hands and owned her with a massive kiss that sent her jumping into his arms.

When she did this, her mounds of tulle hiked up to reveal a pair of white fishnet stockings and knee-high white Chuck Taylors.

As their friends all cheered on the beach, Kai whispered, "I hope you didn't take the pill today. I'm gonna rip those stockings off you and fuck your Ivy League brains out."

She laughed. "Gross image, but I like it."

He carried her down the aisle to the waiting VW van, which was decked out in black, white and tie-dye decorations. She replied, "That's not how birth control works, babe. You have to stop well in advance of trying to get pregnant."

His face fell and his heart nearly broke.

She winked as she adjusted herself in her seat. "Don't worry," she said. "I stopped taking it the day we made up."

"KAI, we have to get to the reception to greet our guests," she said, barely able to catch her breath.

"Not before I get you pregnant first."

Kai had parked the VW at the hotel where their guests were having an extended cocktail hour, but he wasn't letting his bride out of the vehicle just yet.

He intended to thoroughly ravish his woman before the two of them were swept up in the wave of chatting guests and wedding cake.

Zara had been expecting to at least make it to the hotel suite to change into her reception dress—Big Daddy's check for Kai's song had cleared in a big, bad way—but Kai had parked the van in a secluded corner of the lot and dragged her to the back. He had laid down the back seats into a bed, covering it with blankets and sprinkled with black rose petals.

"I'm not taking off my dress out here in a parking lot."

"Then don't," he gritted out, as he laid her back on the cushions. "I don't need to undress you to fuck that smirk off your face."

After he ripped off her stockings, he used one end to tie her wrists together. When she gasped, he whispered, "Too much?"

He gave her a moment to think about it. She bit her lip and blushed, setting off a glow on her skin that looked extra naughty against the white sweetheart neckline of her dress.

"Tie it tighter …bad boy musician."

He was beyond words, his aching cock making his white linen pants too tight for comfort. He tied the other end of the stockings around an armrest. Kai then lifted her dress and rejoiced at the absence of panties. She was already slick and ready for him. He drank in her pussy with his mouth, working her over until she was on the verge of frenzied pleasure that he knew was all the more intense with her hands tied up over her head.

With one quick surprise move, Kai shifted upward and sank his aching cock into its ultimate relief. Zara felt tight and warm around him. But this was their wedding day, and he wanted to take it to the next level. Kai took both of Zara's legs in his arms and placed them on his shoulders, holding her steady while he continued to thrust into her without missing a beat.

The new sensation paid off quickly, with the surprise transition sending Zara closer the edge sooner. Her spasms of pleasure pushed him over the edge, and soon he was coming deep inside.

When he finished, he untied her hands and they lay

pretzeled together, their wedding clothes soiled, sweaty and wrinkled. They laughed and wondered exactly how they were going to make their entrance now.

"Hey," he said. "If Mick Jagger can screw between the set list and the encore, we can, too."

She laughed. "Did that really happen?"

Kai chuckled, "Who knows, but it seems possible."

"Everyone will know what we've been doing."

He winked. "What's more rock and roll than that?"

Epilogue

T_en years later_

THE PHONE at Vinyl Vixen was ringing off the hook.

Meanwhile, Zara was trying and failing to persuade the nine-year-old twins, Jett and Jagger, to put their shoes on, because Great-Aunt Jo was coming to pick them up in five minutes.

"Hello, Vinyl Vixen," she said, cradling the phone between her ear and her shoulder and gesturing wildly to her lackadaisical twins, pointing them to their shoes.

Why they run around the store barefoot is anybody's guess, but probably because they take after their hippie father.

"Hey, congrats on the write-up in *Rolling Stone*; the hipsters are gonna descend on your store like flies on shit any day now."

Zara shook her head and smiled. "Hey, Jed."

The famous magazine had recently ranked Vinyl Vixen

as one of the top ten hidden record store treasures in the nation, adding a mention that songwriter Kai Stormcloud had gotten his start here when a certain ultra-famous musician had walked into the store one day and heard him playing.

"The story isn't 100 percent correct, but I'm not going to sneeze about it," she said with a chuckle. "How's Ma?"

"She does not like Icelandic food; I'll leave it at that. Otherwise, she's in her element. Especially the part where she gets to tell groupies to fuck off and leave me alone."

Zara laughed. "Yes, I can see my mother enjoying that part very much."

Jed asked, "Where is my young ingenue, by the way? I have an idea for a song and I thought he might like to co-write it with me."

She looked around the store. "Hell, if I knew where Kai was at right now, I wouldn't be doing the frazzled mommy act. I'll have him call you, but I'm gonna go ahead and say yes, he'll do it."

"Who needs a manager when they got a wife who can lay a record exec to waste with one cocky attitude, am I right?"

Zara smirked. It was nice to be well thought of by at least one old man in this world. "I take that as a high compliment, Big Daddy. When you're right, you're right."

"Bye for now, and stop calling me that, would ya?"

She smiled and hung up the phone just as another call came in. Out of nowhere, Kai grabbed the phone out of her hand and said, "Vinyl Vixen is closed to celebrate Kai and Zara's tenth anniversary, which will include leaving all manner of DNA in the listening booth. See you in three days!"

He hung up the phone and tossed it aside, then grabbed Zara around the waist and hoisted her up on the counter. He embraced her with abandon and laid a kiss on her that made her purr, and almost made her forget their kids were in the room.

"Eeew!"

Almost. The chorus of two was watching, horrified, as their parents made out like teenagers.

Kai grunted and pulled away from his wife's lips. "Damn kids wouldn't be standing there getting grossed out if they had their DAMN. SHOES. ON. Oh look, Great Aunt Jo is coming up the sidewalk. You two gonna get your shit together and go or what?"

Zara pinched his ass. "You shouldn't swear at the kids like that. They'll get in trouble at school for repeating it."

Kai looked down and cleared his throat. "About that… they kind of already have."

"Oh, for fuck's sake, Kai! You didn't tell me?"

"I hide things in the name of saving your sanity, my love."

Just then, the doorbell rang, now chiming a tinkly version of "Casey Jones." Kai was rather proud of that.

Zara hopped off the counter and trotted over to hug Jo. "Last chance to say no; they are pure evil today."

Jo laughed. "They've got nothing on a nine-year-old Kai. OK, you kids ready?"

After Jett and Jagger finally had their shoes on, Jo led them like little ducklings down the street.

"They sure do fall in line with her around," Kai said, laughing.

Zara locked the door and turned around the sign in the door to read "Closed." Then she turned to her husband with an evil expression. "And as for you…pick your consequence."

Kai hopped over the counter like Spiderman to face

off with Zara. "I'm a grown-ass man. I don't need conse-quences."

She reached up and pulled on the loose-hanging ties on his decades-old baja tunic. "It won't hurt, I promise. A little spanking. A little pinching. Maybe a little biting. A little ripping this tunic to shreds and throwing it on a bonfire on the beach."

He growled. Zara returned the growl with a slap to his ass, then hiked up that god-awful tunic to pinch one of his nipples while biting the other.

Kai moaned at what she was doing to his chest and then freed himself of his tunic altogether. He followed this by pulling off her top, flinging her bra to the floor and diving in between her gorgeous breasts.

She sighed. "I'm glad you still like them, even though they're ten years older and a little saggier after breastfeed-ing. I was thinking about getting them fluffed up a bit over here, tucked in a bit over there…"

He looked up and took her face in his hands. "You fed two babies at once until they were two years old. Your tits are fuckin' rock stars and I won't have you talking smack about 'em."

She rolled her eyes. "What am I gonna do with you?"

Kai peppered her face, neck and chest with kisses as he answered. "Just keep kicking the shit out of my heart; you're stuck with me."

THE END

An Excerpt from the
companion stand-alone
story...

HER HI-FI HUNK

Jed

Ten-plus years, and he still felt the most at home on the wide seaside deck of his neighbors in Santa Barbara.

In between world tours, this is where the god of blues-rock guitar could be found. Drinking beer. Shooting the shit. Listening to the waves and watching the stars. There was nothing else he needed, except maybe someone to make the tour life bearable.

Tonight, his neighbors informed him a friend of theirs would be stopping by. A friend from Sea Grove.

Jed had a strange, uneasy feeling in his gut about this.

His gut was confirmed as he strolled down his private boardwalk, through the gate and up the stairs to Galen and Marti's deck, his six pack of Bud under his arm. He saw the stranger from a distance. A female, 40s, assymetrical wavy hair, nice rack, curves galore, and lots of bangles on her wrists.

It might be her, he thought.

She looked like she could be the same female he'd secretly stalked on social media for years. The same female he'd spoken to briefly on the phone ten years ago when trying to remember the name of a song. The same female who had, via the internet and the U.S. Postal Service, been fulfilling his orders for bootleg recordings of obscure musicians whose records Jed didn't even want. What had he wanted? *A twisted, one-sided romance from afar, perhaps? A fantasy that only needed to be fed with occasional, short email interactions? A friendship based on deceit, because she had no idea of the true identity of her best customer?*

Galen introduced them. "Jed, this is our dear friend Dusty."

She looked at him, and her golden-brown eyes knocked him flat on his ass. Yes, it was her. Dusty Rhodes from the record store down in in Sea Grove. Dusty from the phone call right here on Galen's deck, ten years ago.

She held out her hand to shake his, and her gold bangles of various sizes clanked up and down her forearms. He tried not to stare at her rack, but across it was stretched a burned-out Labyrinth-era David Bowie tee shirt. He had an irrational feeling of jealousy toward Bowie and his familiarity with Dusty's breasts at the moment.

Her haircut was the same as in her pictures from the website, but now instead of brown it was dyed all the colors of the rainbow. A little blue over here, purple over there. She had a beautiful smile and spoke with the same low, sexy voice he had burned into his brain from ten years ago.

He took her hand and it was delicate and warm inside both of Jed's big Irish mitts.

He knew right them he was going to have to step up his game.

Dusty

"Galen and Marti are in trouble, bit time," she said. "They told me their neighbor Jed was coming over to hang out with us. They did not say their neighbor happened to be Jed 'Big Daddy' Masters."

It had been a glorious three days in Santa Barbara. And she was relieved that Marti and Galen were totally on board with keeping the one artifact that Walter would definitely come looking for as soon as his dumb ass was out of prison.

Earlier, Dusty had watched Galen put the famous pair of eyeglasses into the safe and locked it up.

"Thank you, she'd said with a huge sigh of relief. "I can't tell you how much stress this takes off me. I never should have taken it, but I did. I didn't feel safe with it in my store knowing that Walter is going to be out soon."

Galen had waved off any concern she might have felt. "This safe, in this neighborhood? Nobody's touching it. There are plenty of people who like to live here under the radar, and they pay handsomely for it."

Dusty had certainly been intrigued by this comment, but she sure didn't know exactly what that meant.

And now, standing in front of Big Daddy, she did. She was face-to-face with one of those inconspicuous neighbors.

Jed seemed to wince at the term Big Daddy.

Dusty asked him, "Should I not call you that?"

He grinned. "You may call me whatever you like," he said.

He held her hand a little too long. His silvery-blue eyes made contact with hers a little too long. She wasn't sure, but she thought she saw those eyes of his drift down her neck, and further down. If she wasn't mistaken, well, she could go home and tell Zara that the rock god himself seemed to like her rack.

Dusty studied Jed for a moment, trying to tamp down her inner star-stricken fangirl. Finally, Galen commented, "he's lying, he hates that nickname."

Jed was looking at her like she was both the Queen of the Nile and also a piece of meat. Dusty kind of liked the combination. It had been a while since any man had looked at her like that. Or, perhaps they had, and she had never noticed.

Something about that expression and those drifting eyes made her thighs heat up and her her nipples tingle.

She had never experienced anything like that before. Not with the loser criminal Walter. Not with anyone. Jed had a sweet, crooked grin and his eyes crinkled when his smile reached his eyes. His salt and pepper hair was close cropped but still had the hint of the wild waves he wore when he had first come upon the scene decades ago.

Dusty couldn't stop herself from taking a deep breath. She had always wondered what Big Daddy smelled like. She assumed it was a musky combination of sweat and tour bus gasoline.

She was totally wrong.

He smelled like the woods after it rained. Fresh and earthy at the same time.

The whole world knew that Dusty was Ozzy's biggest fan. What they didn't know was guitar playing like Jed's could knock her panties off in a hot second, no questions asked.

No wine, dinner or foreplay necessary.

Dusty would take one look at his record jackets and cream herself every time.

And now that she was meeting him in person, she felt electrified.

And also, a little pissed at her friends.

Marti, her best friend since they were in high school drama together, handed Dusty a glass of pinot grigio and said, "Funny story, I think you two may have talked on the phone once or twice and not even realized it."

Dusty broke her eye contact with the amazing Big Daddy and looked at Marti. "What are you talking about?"

Marti turned to Galen who took over telling the story.

"Yeah, that's right. Hey, Jed. Remember that night you were over here about, I don't know eight or ten years ago, and you were trying to remember the name of a song? And we called up our friend with the record shop?"

Dusty's gaze went from Marti to Galen to Jed.

Something weird was going on behind Jed's eyes. "Yeah," Jed said, warily.

"Well," Galen continued, "This is her. This is Dusty, she of Vinyl Vixen fame."

Jed raised his eyebrows in fake surprise.

Dusty, though, was genuinely shocked.

"Wait a minute. That was you?" she asked.

Jed shrugged and said, "guilty."

Dusty stared at the man, her mouth fallen open. Galen and Marti's conversation became background noise. She studied Jed's face.

He was the one.

Ever since that phone call ten years ago, when some poor friend of Galen and Marti's had been subjected to Dusty's sarcastic pre-teen daughter Zara's comments, her record sales had gone from weak to steady.

A man calling himself "J from Santa Barbara" had started ordering music from her about once a month. Sometimes he would order entire collections. The entire

The Who discography. Beatles. Stones. Sometimes it was recordings that were very difficult to track down, and she charged him a bundle. He had never tried to talk the price down.

This whole time. It wasn't just "J" from Santa Barbara. Her whole life had been propped up by none other than Jed Fucking Big Daddy Masters; as if he were her goddamn sugar daddy for the past ten years.

Holy shit.

About the Author

Abby Knox lives a dual life. Fantasy Abby would love to live on a farm with goats, bees, chickens, donkeys and alpaca, making her own soap, yarn, honey and cheese, and spend her free time arguing about music with Jack Black. Reality Abby has no desire to do actual farm work and Jack Black just won't return her calls. So, the ever-pragmatic Reality Abby keeps Fantasy Abby happy by putting her into sweet little works of romantic pastoral fiction with her pretend hobbies. Both Abbies hope you enjoy this brand of sweet, sexy, storytelling. This is Abby's twelfth book.

Keep up with the latest news with Abby's newsletter!
Say hello at
authorabbyknox@gmail.com